The Pot Job

Praise for Bart Schaneman

"Here is an incomplete list of things Bart Schaneman knows well: the aimlessness of a quarter life crisis in America, weed, the confusion that happens when you have it all figured out, day drinking, the uncertain entanglements of love and friendship, Denver, the definition of a cannagar, hipster bars, the tragedy of traveling the world and coming home feeling hollow, post-crime paranoia, low-wage labor jobs, strip clubs. What's most impressive isn't that Bart knows these things, but the way he imbues his characters with this knowledge so seamlessly and realistically—and God, is it good to read a book that celebrates the beautiful mess of being alive."

**Mason Parker,
author of *Until the Red Swallows It All***

"At the intersection of legal cannabis and criminal enterprise, Schaneman captures the marijuana industry with nuance. Yet, it's less of a book about weed and more a book that grapples with questions of integrity. *The Pot Job* is one of those rare novels where you both want to lick your fingers to turn the pages faster while also slowing down to savor every word."

**Wendy J. Fox,
author of *What If We Were Somewhere Else***

"*The Pot Job* rolls us into a plot full of dark humor and vivid characters worth rooting for despite the fuckery hidden behind the haze of smoke band shenanigans. Schaneman has created a tastier slice of Americana worth every ounce."

**Hillary Leftwich,
author of *Aura* and *Saint Dymphna's Playbook***

"Bart Schaneman's writing crackles like a live wire knocked down from the pole and sparking in the street. His voice is a voice of the earth--lean, evocative, true, elemental. Like Didion and Steinbeck, Bart's fiction serves as its own sort of history and will one day be seen as a substantial document of How We Were."

Adam Gnade,
author of *After Tonight, Everything Will Be Different*

"Schaneman blends generational ethos like fine soil."

Bram Riddlebarger,
author of *Western Erotica Ho*

ISBN: 978-1-951226-23-7

Cover design by Rachel Pfeffer

Published by Trident Press
940 Pearl St.
Boulder, CO 80302

tridentcafe.com/trident-press-titles

THE POT JOB

by Bart Schaneman

Trident Press
Boulder, CO

Taylor Hobson stepped over the rubble and went into the office. She sat in a swivel chair and watched security footage on the monitors, starting at midnight and fast-forwarding until she saw the truck with the bull bar smash through the wall. She leaned forward, the monitor light glowing in the dark room, and felt sick, forcing herself to breathe.

The black and white video made the robbery look fake —a Buster Keaton film, minus the vaudeville soundtrack. The truck reversed and two guys in black, hooded sweatshirts stepped through the wreckage. With their headlamps, masks, and backpacks, they moved with purpose, quickly finding what they were after. Each one grabbed a plastic tote full of trimmed marijuana and hauled it out of the frame.

Taylor rubbed her eyes with the heels of her hands and made herself sit up. She had expected something like this to happen at some point, but she wasn't ready for it right now.

The robbers made at least three trips. One broke the glass of a display case and leaned in to snatch a dab rig. His partner, who was dragging his left foot, grabbed him and pulled him toward the back. They went to the vault and stood in front of it for a minute, looking back and forth at each other, gesturing and arguing. They walked out and Taylor expected them to come back with an acetylene torch or a handtruck to haul the whole thing out, but nothing more happened on the video until a cop showed up with his flashlight, more than 30 minutes later.

Taylor played it back and watched it at 2x speed. She filmed it with her phone and posted it to the company Instagram account with a caption offering a $500 reward for information. She put the merchandise that was left into the vault, locked the office, and went out to the street.

She sat on her motorcycle, pausing before putting on her helmet. Yellow police caution tape encircled the store.

"Fuck," she said under her breath. Pot shops couldn't get insurance. The cops weren't on their side. They'd have to make the money back on their own. Then she had an idea.

She had friends back home who still worked in the black market and were earning a lot more money than she ever could selling legal weed. No taxes or regulations in the illicit market. Her friends would love to sell the Colorado weed she was growing, and she had other cultivation operations she could borrow from. It was the best way to make up the money they'd lost. She'd just need to figure out a way to get the cannabis there without getting caught.

She started the bike, cranked the throttle, and shot away down the street—her thin frame wrapped over the machine. Hours before, the skyline had glittered with fireworks, but now the Denver streets were tired, bleary-eyed, the city not awake, not quite asleep. Traffic wobbled around her. She weaved past cars at high speed. Rolled through lights and stop signs. The early morning air peeled away her drowsiness.

At home Danielle was sitting cross legged in bed scrolling through her feeds on her phone, looking for any news. Her black hair was up—sharp features drawn tight.

"Nice video," she said. "Would be better if it wasn't our shop."

Taylor sat down and stared at the floor. "Understatement of the year. We lost so much money."

"What did the cops say?"

"About what you'd expect. Nothing really. No help. I have an idea. It's pretty crazy, but it might work."

Taylor went into the bathroom and turned on the shower. She was thinking this might be it. Only a year in and already failed at owning their own business before they had a chance to really get started. They weren't the only pot shop who had gotten hit lately. Marijuana companies couldn't use banks because weed was federally illegal and most convenience stores had stopped carrying much cash, so criminals figured the cannabis industry was a soft target. It had been happening all over the city.

By early morning, Taylor's surveillance video post had received dozens of comments. The bulk of them were sympathetic, if not constructive. Most said some form of "That sucks," or "People like this should be shot." The direct messages had more utility. One, from a regular trimmer named Greg, said, "I'm pretty sure I know who that is. He used to work for you." Taylor was at the kitchen island thumbing through her phone while she drank her coffee. She direct messaged Greg. "Call me immediately."

He called and said one guy in the video might be named Kevin. He had worked for their business Sugar Magnolia on the seasonal harvest and trim crew until the weekend of the robbery, when he had stopped showing up for work. "I can't see his face perfectly," Greg said. "But I'm pretty sure it's him. Wrecked his bike a couple of weeks ago. You can see him limping."

"You sure this is the guy?"

"Pretty sure. He was living over on Colfax and Race. A bunch of dudes hang out there. Always talking right-wing bullshit. Wouldn't shut up with their conspiracy theories."

Taylor hung up and called Nick. He was working security and driving for Sugar Magnolia. She explained to him what had happened and what she wanted to do. "Should be pretty straightforward. Let's get our weed back."

"This kind of shit's never straightforward."

"I'll give you twenty percent of the value of anything we recover. As a bonus."

Taylor waited a beat for him to respond.

"All right. Come pick me up."

2.

____

Nick lived with two guys on Inca Street in the Golden Triangle. He rented a room in a blue Victorian two-level house with white trim and fishscale woodwork layered on the eaves. His roommates were part of an ex-military group using medical marijuana as an experimental treatment program to help with PTSD after their service in Afghanistan.

When Taylor pulled up Nick was sitting on the front steps scanning the traffic. Thick-necked, buzzcut, dark sleeves of tattoos on both arms. He hopped up and came to the passenger window.

"How heavy do we think this is going to get?" he asked.

"Not heavy at all. You being here should be enough."

"I can bring some toys if we think we need them."

"No. No fucking toys. Jesus. Let's go."

Nick got in and sat up straight, on high alert as Taylor drove. It was about noon, the sky cloudless and so blue it was almost white. Taylor stopped at a light and with her window down she felt the heat rising from the concrete.

"My contact said these guys are Proud Boys," Taylor said. "Or Proud Boy wannabes. Boogaloo bullshit. That kind of thing."

"In that case, we should have brought masks. They love mace."

"They'll see you, a real soldier, and shit their pants."

Nick being there was reassuring—she didn't love conflict.

She drove down old Colfax, passed the stone cathedral, the music venues, and the tent camps on the sidewalks. The corner bar she used to love had boarded up windows after gunshots shattered all the glass and the owners abandoned it. One of many that way. She turned right on Race, driving slowly.

"That's the place," Nick said, pointing to a bungalow with a sign in the living room window showing a weathervane surrounded by a circle of bullets. They parked behind a white van with a bumper sticker of a unicorn holding an assault rifle. Before Taylor could confer with Nick on their plan of attack, he was across the street pounding on the front door, Taylor hustling to catch up.

When the lock turned and the door began to open Nick shouldered it, knocking someone down.

"Hey man, what the fuck?" the guy said from the floor.

Taylor went in after Nick, already feeling a rush of adrenaline, her heart rate and breathing elevated.

Nick stood over the skinny, blue-hoodie-clad young man. A small tattoo of the face of a cartoon frog next to his left eye. "Which one of you is Kevin?"

Two guys came down the stairs and through the kitchen, one with a meat tenderizer, the other a frying pan. They held the cookware up but stopped when they saw Nick.

The muscles in his jaw pulsed as he watched them. The back of his neck and ears flushed deep red. "You want to put all that shit down," he said.

The two guys stood there with their kitchen items, shifting their weight back and forth. The skinny guy on the floor glanced around the room.

"Tell this one to stop looking around," Nick said into the kitchen.

"Man, fuck you," the skinny guy said, getting to his feet. "Get out of our fucking house."

Nick took two strides, grabbed him by the sweatshirt and headbutted him, sounding like thumping a watermelon.

He let him go and the guy dropped to the floor, holding his nose.

The guys looked at their bleeding friend and set their utensils on the counter.

"Do you mind if I have a seat?" Taylor asked. She sat on the edge of a tattered red recliner.

"You must be Kevin, right?" She pointed to the one on the floor, noticing his foot was in a walking boot.

"You want your weed back? That shit is in Iowa or wherever. Who the fuck knows?"

"Of all the places to rob, why my store? Why where you work? That's so stupid."

"It's just a way to get money for supplies—weapons and tear gas, shit like that."

"What, to fight antifa?" Nick asked.

"They don't fight fair," Kevin said.

"They don't fight fair," Nick said, matching his whiny tone.

Kevin was holding his nose, blood running through his fingers. He picked up his phone and started to dial a number when Nick stepped over and kicked him in the frog tattoo. His head snapped back and bounced off the floor. Nick went to the coat rack on the wall and took a key ring off a hook.

"That's not our van," the one with the meat tenderizer said. "You're going to have to at least hit me."

"Not a problem. You want to do the honors?"

"I'd rather not," Taylor said.

"Do it, bitch," the guy said.

Nick took a breath then kneed him in the gut. When he slumped over he hit him in the eye with an overhand right. The guy went down.

"That's probably enough," Taylor said. "Oh shit."

Kevin stood in the corner, quiet, holding his nose with one hand and a can of pepper spray in the other. His eyes were feral. A caged animal hopping on one foot.

"Don't be stupid," Nick said, moving toward him.

The guy mumbled behind his hand something that sounded like *just fucking leave*.

"We're not even," Nick said as they walked out. "Don't ever come by one of our stores. I'll burn this place down."

Outside, Taylor squinted. The city was supercharged, bright and loud. Nick jogged to the van, got in, and took off.

Inside her car, Taylor's hands were shaking. Not a panic attack but something close to it. She wished for a second she still smoked. Her legs shook the whole way back to the main office.

In the parking lot, Nick pulled in behind her and Danielle came out to meet them as they walked up to the warehouse. By then, Taylor's energy levels were crashing. She was exhausted, but she grabbed a Leatherman from the storage shed, took off the van's license plates, unscrewed one from the front of their work truck, and put it on the back of the new vehicle.

"Where'd we get the van?" Danielle asked. "And why are you bleeding?"

"I'm going to go wash this blood off my head," Nick said.

"Is someone going to tell me what happened?"

"We didn't get our weed, but we got something better. I think we can do this," Taylor said. "I told Nick the plan. You're going to hate it."

3.

The wind blew from the north, carrying a faint aroma of the dog food factory over the city. Denver natives said the smell meant it was going to rain. Taylor stood in front of the open back doors of the white panel van with the unicorn bumper sticker. Danielle and her had finished loading it to the top with gray plastic tote bins full of marijuana bud. It was after midnight, the sky clear enough despite the moon and light pollution, the Big Dipper obvious above them.

"Let's get going," Taylor said.

Danielle wore her dark hair in a ponytail. Silver light-weight down puffy jacket and black leggings. Brand new Nike running shoes with glowing white bottoms. She closed the van doors and with a cordless drill screwed on the blue-and-white plate with an outline of The Sower statue from the top of the Nebraska capitol building. It was an old one she had kept as a souvenir when they moved to Colorado, and she hoped it would get them through the state.

Under their jackets they both wore the T-shirts they typically wore to the Husker bar in Capitol Hill for football games.

"Go Big Red," Danielle said, as she got in and pulled on her seat belt.

"If we make it, I'm buying you a steak and a milkshake," Taylor said.

"We'll make it."

The drive started smoothly enough. Danielle drove east and they listened to public radio on I-76 until they came to Fort Morgan, where the sugar beet factory reminded Taylor of home. When the signal faded they switched to AM and listened to talk radio. A man with a voice like it was being broadcast from some subterranean bunker ranted about the 2nd Amendment of the Constitution, how it was possible certain school shootings were staged by anti-gun activists. That even with a Republican president in office their guns were not safe. "I've heard from many listeners about a knock on the door in the middle of the night from men in suits who come in and confiscate. They confiscate in the name of Homeland Security, and you're powerless to stop them. This country was built on certain inalienable rights, freedoms..."

Then over the flat land along the North Platte River. Under the moonlight the fields were dark with tall corn and lighter where there was wheat. Spots of black cattle frozen motionless on the hillocks of pastureland. The straight, gray interstate highway carried on ahead blue and endless.

"I'm so bored," Taylor said from the passenger seat. "Let's get stoned."

"The van smells enough like weed already."

"I'll roll my window down." Taylor lit a joint and puffed on it until the cherry glowed hot and red. She passed it to Danielle; she hit it and coughed.

As the pot took effect, they settled into the highway noise, leaning into their seats, relaxed. They drove on with the windows cracked until Danielle pulled over at a rest stop next to a grove of cottonwoods. "Either we stop and sleep or you drive."

Taylor got out and stretched her arms as she shuffled into the bathroom. The overhead lights buzzed, harsh brightness reflecting off the tiled floor. A Latina woman emerged from the handicapped stall and put up a yellow Wet Floor stand. Taylor nodded and the woman nodded back.

She bought a Diet Coke from the vending machine on

the way out. She never drank pop, but this was a special occasion. No way she could risk falling asleep.

Danielle was curled up in her seat, dozing off, before Taylor had even driven five miles.

About two hours later, Taylor was meditating on the white highway lines and the voice on the radio when she saw an electric highway sign on the shoulder that read K-9 DRUG UNIT AHEAD. She sat up and said, "Oh shit. Fuck."

Danielle woke up with a whimper. "What? What's happening?"

"Sign said drug dog ahead."

Taylor turned on her signal and exited off the interstate.

"Let's take the old highway."

When she crested the hill a highway patrol car sat parked on the shoulder. There was no immediate town here, not many reasons to take this exit. Taylor hit the brakes, but the trooper flipped on his lights as they passed.

"Fuck," Taylor said, watching from the side mirror as the cop pulled onto the road. "It's a trap. Fuck this."

"Babe, what did you do?"

"Hang on."

With the gas pedal all the way down, Taylor turned sharp and skidded onto the first dirt road she came across, hoping the corn would help hide the dust long enough for her to make a few more turns. From the mirrors, red and blue light shaded the edges of the dust. It could be a lot darker. The moon cast the scene in a dim glow. She turned at intersection after intersection until they were deep into the farm fields. After another turn brought them across the end of a soybean field, Danielle turned and said, "I don't see him."

"I'm not slowing down."

In another mile, the dirt road curved then rose over a railroad crossing. Taylor chose not to let up, and the van caught air as it jumped the tracks. The road curved back again and as they landed and hit the dirt Taylor lost control. The van skidded off the road and jumped the ditch. The bins in the back jostled and came open, the buds bouncing around in the back like popcorn popping. They came to a stop as the bumper plowed into the riverbank. Taylor leaned forward. Water rushed by the front of the vehicle. She tried to reverse, but they were high-centered.

"We gotta go. Grab anything with our names on it," Taylor said.

As Danielle gathered her things, Taylor scurried to the back and used her knife to unscrew the license plate. She flung it into the river where it landed with a slap.

They ran across the road into tall corn, the field humid and wet. The ground was soft from the sprinkler with a slippery layer of topsoil mud that collected on the soles of their shoes. They stopped and waited, trying to listen over their panting. On the other side of the field, water hit the leaves from the center pivot and all they could hear was the chuck-chuck-chuck of the end gun.

After a few minutes, a cop car arrived. From where they stood they could only see a sliver of the van. The officer spotlit the field and the light shone across the top of the corn. The intercom squawked with unintelligible commands. The cop parked and got out.

Danielle turned into the field and began to walk.

"I was trying to get away." Taylor pleaded.

"Let's just get the fuck out of here," Danielle said.

Their profits destined to rot in some police storage facility, they walked single file down the dark cornrows. The leaves scratched their faces and necks and hands as they went along. Taylor's phone picked up a weak signal. The map app showed a town she had never heard of six miles ahead. This was a blank, unfamiliar part of the state, one you wouldn't visit without good reason. From the outline on the screen, the town looked too small to have a hotel or much pedestrian traffic of any kind.

"We can't just walk out of a random cornfield in the middle of nowhere," Taylor called up to Danielle. "I'll call Nick."

"Nick's surfing in Mexico. Call Wesley and tell him to come get us. He likes you better."

Taylor called. Wesley, their vice president of operations at Sugar Magnolia, had been sleeping. She gave him the situation. "Can't you rent a car?" he said.

"We're in the middle of nowhere. Plus, we're pretty hot. I'll send you a pin."

They emerged from the field and followed a ditch to the edge of town. Looking down the main street, the town could have been any other dried-up farm town. The old stone courthouse was the only building of any size. The other buildings—retail shops, a feed store, and a diner—could have been from the '50s, if not older. Nothing was open. One pickup in the distance moved slowly down the highway.

They came upon an abandoned factory—a red brick building with broken windows, a smokestack, and silos, the lot around it overgrown. Plastic bags caught in the Kochia weed. They walked to it and found a place to rest in the doorway of one of the outer buildings.

The light in the east brightened as they waited. They could watch the highway from where they sat and one state trooper passed by, then another. Traffic picked up by the hour. On the farm down the road, a tractor inched along, smoke rising from the stack when the farmer throttled up after turning around at the end of the field.

"Somebody's going to see us," Danielle said.

"Text him," Taylor said. "My phone's about dead."

Danielle sent: "What's your ETA?"

No response. A few hours ago, Taylor had dropped a pin when they found the factory and Wesley responded with a thumbs up, but he hadn't texted since. As the pre-dawn light shone brighter, a few more cars and trucks moved in and out of town.

Behind them, the sun cast long shadows over the fields, and a gaudy, oversized SUV turned off the highway, coming toward them. It was the color of a pearl and shined on the dirt road, obvious and out of place.

"Thank god," Taylor said. "Stay low."

The truck stopped at the entrance of the factory road. They ran to Wesley and hopped in the backseat.

"What the fuck happened?" Wesley asked. His sharp-angled face was tired under his black and gray trucker hat.

"Drive, drive, drive," Taylor said.

"Thank fuck you're here," Danielle said.

"Where's the van?" The car drove smooth and quiet as Wesley pulled onto the empty highway.

"Don't take the interstate," Taylor said. "They're looking for us. We just saw the cops."

"I would really like to know what's going on."

"Hold on. We'll tell you. Just want to make sure we're good," Taylor said.

They drove in silence for a while, both Taylor and Danielle glancing out the side and rear windows for any sign they were being followed.

"Who's going to tell me what happened?"

"Fucking horrible. Easily the worst night of my life," Danielle said.

"Agreed."

"Is someone going to tell me what the hell is going on?"

Taylor's eyes were tired. She gave him a very simple explanation that they were chased through the fields by the cops.

"That's it? How did they know what you were doing?"

"We're wiped out," Danielle said, slumping against the door. "Can we tell you all the details later?"

"Yes, please. Just drive and don't speed," Taylor said.

As they slept, Wesley came up with a list of insults he could hurl at them, but they were signing his checks. He tried to appreciate the view of the plains. Here the sky was clear, not overcast from the wildfires. He hadn't been in deep rural country for a long time.

He pulled in for gas at a town on the Colorado border. Taylor woke up surprised by how badly she needed to pee and shuffled across the parking lot to the store.

Wesley caught Danielle's red eyes in the rearview mirror. He waited for her to say something. She picked up her phone, charging on a cable from the center console, and scrolled. Wesley got out and slammed his door. He had about five gallons in when Danielle set her phone down and went around the car and asked if he wanted her to pump the gas.

"I got it," he said. He turned his back to her and pulled the squeegee from the plastic box on the pillar, dirty blue liquid dripping on the cement.

About 30 miles outside Denver, pink and orange wildfire glow radiated up from the horizon. The forest west of Golden had been burning for three days and the smoke and fire turned the sky the color of dusk, as though the sun was setting. It was 12:30 in the afternoon. People pulled over on the shoulder to take pictures with their phones. He opened Instagram and filmed a five second story. An early July wildfire and so far east of the forest.

"I'm guessing if the fire had made it to Denver, my phone would have told me by now," Taylor said. "I guess we keep going."

When Wesley got to Taylor and Danielle's house he went to the back door of the car and flung it open. Danielle nearly fell on the ground. Taylor mumbled a soft thanks and tried to hug him. He side-stepped her, got in, and left without waiting for them to make it in.

Inside, their two rescue dogs—Jack, a merle mutt of unknowable breeds, and Louie, a French bulldog mix—spun around in place and jumped up to lick their hands. Jack ran in and out through the dog door. Taylor filled their bowls with food and water and told them to calm down.

She slept next to Danielle through the afternoon until the bedroom grew too hot, the air stale, the sheets damp.

She showered and made coffee and sat out on the balcony listening to the music of the city. She was not at all sure they would get away with it.

She was changing into nicer pants when Danielle woke up. "Where are you going? I'm so tired."

"Work. Sounds like Wesley needs some help. The Evans store's out of cash. And Federal can't get its POS to work."

"Take the day off. It'll be fine."

Danielle was right—Wesley could handle it, but Taylor said, "I need to do something. Can't just stay here."

She left Danielle sitting up in bed, looking at her phone.

4.

———————————

A black Camry with an Uber sticker in the back window stopped in front of a modern, blocky, flat-roofed house. The sun had dropped behind the horizon and shade covered the neighborhood in a cool stillness. A guy in his late 20s stepped out of the car and pulled a blue camping backpack and tan laptop bag from the trunk. He shouldered both and walked toward the house in cracked black cowboy boots, a black T-shirt, and cheap gray jeans. He was lean with strong arms and a full head of unwashed, sandy blonde hair. Eyes blood-shot from flying.

Taylor sat on a wooden stool on the porch and played an acoustic guitar with a sticker on it that said EAT THE RICH. She wore jeans under a white cotton dress and a red headband to hold back her brown hair. Her skin was clear and she looked healthy. Not too thin. Strong. A little tired around her mouth and eyes. The song had a percussive rhythm and she knocked on the body of the guitar as she worked out the words. He watched her with a smile until she realized he was there. "Henry!" she said, setting down her guitar and running to the gate to meet him with a hug.

"I might smell like I've been on three straight airplanes," he said. "It took 24 hours to get here. Well, two months. But a day of airports."

"You actually don't look that tired." She took his laptop

bag from him. "Your trip seemed great. The pictures you posted were amazing."

"Can't wait to tell you all about it." He followed her into the house. The dogs scratched at the hardwood floor and skittered underfoot.

Taylor led him down to his room, which was walled with blankets that hung from the unfinished ceiling. An American flag covered the sunken window well. It was cool and dark and smelled of dirt.

"You can use this desk to write or whatever," she said, pointing to a workman's table scattered with parts from broken-down guitars under a naked lightbulb. "I'll let you get settled in."

"I'd better not stay down here or I'll sleep for three days." He tossed his backpack on the bed, grabbed a couple of bottles from the pouch at the top, and followed her upstairs.

In the living room, Danielle was lying on the couch watching a show about cowboys from a hundred years ago. She turned it off and stood to give him a hug. Henry held up a bottle of soju and another of raspberry wine. He set them down on the coffee table and said, "Come here, Dani. Man, how long's it been?"

"I heard you've been out traveling the world," she said, giving him a hug. "Glad you're back."

Taylor put the soju in the freezer and lined up shot glasses on the kitchen table.

He knew finances were tight in that house. Taylor had told them they'd put all their money into starting the cannabis company and didn't have much cash. But he had just returned to the States and wanted to enjoy at least a few days before he started scraping by. He had about $3,000 left after all his traveling. They should go out, he announced. Drinks were on him.

After the soju shots and a quick shower they walked to a restaurant down the hill. The place had three dining areas, a front and back bar, and an outdoor patio. They ordered plates of vegan spaghetti and meatballs, pizza, and salad, drinking high-alcohol IPAs brewed a few neighborhoods over. To Henry, this was perfect. Food and drinks and friends he missed. Exactly what he wanted on his first night back in the country.

"I love this. Being back in America. In my home country. With my friends. I'm happy," Henry said.

"Why are you talking like that?" Taylor asked.

"Like what?" Henry asked, cutting a tofu meatball with his fork.

"All slow like that. Over-enunciating. You're explaining everything you're saying."

"Fuck. Am I? Traveler's English. From being around too many people who don't speak fluently. I. Am. Speaking. English. Can. You. Understand. My. English?"

"It makes you sound like a dick," Danielle said. She picked the arugula leaves from a slice of pizza. "But it's hilarious."

"Well, would a dick buy a round of whiskey?"

"A dick would not," Taylor said.

They took shots of Maker's Mark.

"God bless America," he said. "Land of cheap, good bourbon. I don't know if I should stick around, but this makes me happy."

"So ... we're kind of in a lot of trouble," Taylor said.

"How so?"

"Did you see we got robbed?" Danielle said.

"I did see that. On Instagram. Did you find the assholes?"

"That happened, then we kind of overreacted," Taylor said. They told him about the van and what happened in Nebraska.

"Holy shit," Henry said. "I didn't know you two had it in you."

"We don't," Taylor said. "We're terrified. I'm so paranoid right now. I keep thinking people are following us. If you see me constantly checking my phone it's because I'm googling 'white van marijuana Nebraska' all the time."

"We might be going to jail," Danielle said.

"We are *definitely* going to jail," Taylor said.

"But probably not tonight," Henry said.

"Probably not tonight," Danielle said.

They finished the meal then walked up the street to Colfax. Henry noticed the amount of space in this American neighborhood. The gaps between the houses. The yards. How far back the buildings were set from the street.

"Everything's so square and neat here. You know they always talk about 'fresh eyes' when you come back from being gone for a while," he said. "It's kind of cool to see all of this like I've never seen it before."

They walked quiet until the clack of a shifter changing gears and the low hum of a vintage road bicycle in the bike lane came up behind them, a young woman with brown curly hair pouring out of her white plastic helmet, a messenger bag strapped around her back, the blue and red striped dress flapping up around her seat.

"It's good to be home," Henry said. "Back in this monster."

They walked past a McDonald's with a Now Hiring sign on the marquee missing a few letters. NO RING, it read, lit up now in the full dark. They passed the capitol and the civic center, with its tent camps in the lawn. To see a guy about his age—in decent health, sitting in a camping chair with a beard and neck tattoos, talking to another guy with his head sticking out of a tent, both drinking 40s of malt liquor—felt heavy and sad.

"We're taking you to our new favorite place," Danielle said.

"Some of the dancers used to be Suicide Girls," Taylor said. "You remember that website."

"Didn't they open for Metallica?"

"It's fun. A party," Danielle. "Not weird or creepy. Not a sad Lincoln strip club."

"Danielle has a crush."

"Whatever you're into. I'm in for the full tour."

The doorman had dark tattoos running up his neck, hoop earrings lining the edges of both ears and a Kevlar vest. He checked their IDs, and they walked into the noise and smells of a very busy place. Men and women sat at the bar and at the stage with the dancers, guys with their girlfriends at the tables. People not just staring at the women but genuinely having fun. It might be more like a cabaret, but Henry wasn't really sure what that meant. He bought a round of beers and they took them to the edge of the stage and sat down.

Cricket was finishing her first dance to a song by the New York Dolls. The next song came on, White Zombie, and she took a hold of the pole and paused. She wore her ginger hair down to her chin. Her skin stretched across her collarbones and out to delicate, rounded shoulders, both fully inked in intricate forest scenes, with fairies and dragonflies and other woodland creatures down to her elbows. She hooked one leg around the pole and held it with her right hand. As the tempo sped up she spun quicker. She climbed and hung and crawled to them. She did a slow walk on her hands and knees to each paying customer, picking up the bills with her hands, her feet, her breasts.

When she got to their group Danielle tucked a bill in Cricket's underwear and said, "That's the luckiest dollar bill in America right now."

Cricket laughed a kind of false laugh and sat back, setting her legs on Dani's shoulders.

After Cricket it was Sunny, who had black hair punctuated by a shock of blonde, more tribal tattoos and deep lines around her mouth. She struggled to find the energy to finish her song. A forced smile. Little eye contact with her customers. But she knew the tricks and how to get paid.

"We're having a blast," Taylor said, a little tipsy.

Henry watched as these two women he'd known since they were teenagers treated each other with real love. It was in their posture and the way they looked at one another and in how they talked. In how they listened. Other people don't really listen to the person speaking—they judge what's being said or wait to make a joke—these two listened to the other speak as though the most banal utterances were the truest words ever spoken. When they were talking they were the only person in the room. He was happy for them.

"Love is all we have," he said.

They weren't so clueless they couldn't include him in the conversation. They asked him about his travels and he told them stories about the real floating mountains he'd found in China, about riding horses on bad saddles with the nomadic tribes in Mongolia, about finding himself in the backseat of a souped-up Mazda in a street race in Russia. They listened and laughed at the right parts, and he could tell he was the entertainment for the date they were on. The date they might be on for the rest of their life. He hoped that was true.

On the walk back to the house, Henry tried to sing an old Bruce Springsteen song, one that had been on the radio, and Danielle said, "Oh hell no. No. Nobody wants to hear that. Taylor, you sing." And she sang them a few bars of a song by The Lumineers. "When we were young, oh oh we did enough..." Henry was carried away by the night and these people and this city—his old favorite feeling.

He woke in darkness early, jet lag sleep disruption. He thumbed at his phone for a while before he sat up and pulled on the light bulb string overhead. The basement was cold and damp. He dug in his pack for a fresh pair of clothes and got dressed. He wanted to write about the trip he had just taken while it was fresh, so he sat at the table and wrote freehand in a pocket notebook until the sun rose and he could hear them moving upstairs.

It was Saturday, and Taylor was out back in a black T-shirt with the sleeves torn off—on one shoulder a black ink tattoo of a Taurus sign, the other one was new, some unknown symbol. She was working on a song about their hometown. Henry walked out into the sun and stretched. Taylor worked through a chord progression for another minute, then she set her guitar down and said, "Breakfast." The dogs stopped pacing the back fence, stopped trying to get at the squirrels in the tree overhead, and followed Henry and Taylor inside.

They sat at the kitchen table and ate blackberries on bowls of plain yogurt and drank black coffee. They spoke softly—Danielle was still sleeping. Taylor was quiet in the morning before she'd had her caffeine. Henry hadn't recovered fully from his jet lag, had woken up in the middle of the night as though he'd taken a four-hour nap.

"Let me get you another cup," Taylor said. "Meet me on the front porch. I need to tell you something."

Sunlight poured down from the east. They sat with their sunglasses on in wicker chairs looking across the street at the Planned Parenthood parking lot. Bored anti-abortion protesters milled about on the sidewalk holding posters with pictures of aborted fetuses.

"So this is going to be a little weird to hear," Taylor said. "But you know Dani and I have been best friends forever. And we're building this business, right?"

Henry sipped at his mug. "You're going to crush it. You're probably already crushing it."

"Yeah, maybe. But the other thing I wanted to tell—"

"You two are dating."

Taylor stood up and turned to lean against the railing. "Is it that obvious?"

"It's obvious. You're not just friends. You finally went to the next level." Henry was smiling now.

"This is a secret." Taylor's face had gotten serious in a gentle, pleading way.

"Anyone with half a brain is going to figure it out."

"It's all really fucked up, I know."

"No, not fucked up at all." Henry held up his mug as a salute. "Good for you."

"It's not what you think. We let each other do what the other person wants. Or whatever. Our only rule is we have to be honest with each other."

"Sounds good in theory."

She turned away from him and looked out at the neighborhood.

He drank the last of his coffee. "Jet lag is a bitch. I'm going to go work out."

Henry changed into silver gym shorts and a white I ♥ Korea T-shirt he had bought at the Incheon airport. The sky was tinted wildfire red. He checked the air quality index on his phone and, with the smoke, Denver's air was more polluted than Seoul's.

As he jogged, he was careful to avoid the buckled paver sections, broken and split from tree roots pushing up underneath. After Asia, to run on quiet, wide streets, past these silent houses with their sprawling gardens and yards, in this greenish city with its abundant, well-cared-for parks and uncrowded open spaces. All so plentiful. He was feeling comfortable. He thought he might even want to stick around for a while.

He ran about a mile out before turning around. His lungs raw. A stitch in his side. Back at the house, Taylor was out on the porch with her guitar.

"That sucked. Hard to breathe at this altitude," he said, panting.

"Show off," she said. She set her phone down and went back to working on a lick.

Henry went inside and was drinking a glass of water with his shirt off. Dani came into the kitchen half asleep and laughed. "You belong in Colorado," she said.

After they all showered and dressed they went to the liquor store, bought two bottles of rosé and took them to the park. A guy on a scooter in knee and elbow pads and a black helmet saw them and said, "Oh hey, real cool! Let's all bring glass bottles to the park!" Dani smiled and said, "Cheers."

They walked until they came to a sloped clearing of grass with a city skyline view and beyond that the low profile of the blue mountains far to the west. Henry had read that people were moving here in droves from all over. They thought Denver was in the mountains, but those mountains were miles away. A rock band practiced on the edge of the park in the pavilion with white Grecian columns. The guitar music washed over them, lapping at their feet and the bottles and the cups they held. A crow flew over the trees, calling as it carried on into the neighborhood.

"Those clouds look like breaking waves," Taylor said, pointing to the horizon where a row of curled clouds formed a perfect set of white breakers against the dark blue sky.

Henry sipped his wine listening to Dani and Taylor. Their conversation ran circles around itself. They would build on the comments made earlier, referencing them again and again, until their sentences had two or three layers of inside jokes and words they had mashed together and manipulated. Funny, but not in an attention-seeking, comedian kind of way. It was good-spirited, alive, positive.

"I need all of you to stand up right now!"

An overweight man in a white polo shirt stretched tight over his chest and belly, khaki shorts bunched up at his thighs, blocked out the sun. They squinted up at him.

"Are you a cop?" Taylor asked.

"The cops haven't been called yet—"

"Then why should we listen to you?"

"—but I need you to stand up and pour out your wine before I call them."

Taylor drank from the bottle. Dani covered up the other one with a blanket.

"Look guys, I used to come up here and do the same thing, drinking in the park," the ranger said. "I hate doing this. If you were a little better at hiding your glass you'd be fine. Pour that out, throw it in the trash, and I'll walk away."

They each finished their cups and Dani handed the guy the empty bottle. "All yours," she said.

"So many fucking rules!" Henry said. "We think we're the freest country in the world, but adults can't drink wine in a park without getting harassed."

They packed up and walked over to a bar—a dark dive in a strip mall next to a pizza place—and ordered another drink.

"What's your plan now?" Dani asked Henry.

"I don't know. I'm trying to write, so I might get a job waiting tables. Some job that doesn't require the same energy. I think my traveling days might be over. Or at least on pause."

"You could work for us," Taylor said.

"Yes! You'd be perfect," Dani said.

"Let me get settled first. See if I can't find my own thing."

They drank and played bar games then walked around the streets of Denver drunk and happy, talking fast and loud about what they wanted from life, ignoring the cost of living, not mentioning getting old, or starting families, but instead talking about places they wanted to see, food they wished they had, and people in their lives they missed.

"I love you two," he said. "This is exactly what I wanted when I came back."

The next evening, Dani drove them west on I-70 at dusk toward a bright red sun setting behind a layer of wildfire smoke. Henry sat in the back and they were quiet, listening to the indie radio station and watching the scenery. The air coming through the vents smelled like they were sitting next to a campfire. They went around the state park outside of Golden and up through homes carved out of the forest.

"How can you live here now?" Danielle said. "Wouldn't you be afraid all the time?"

It was nearly dark when they parked in a line of cars and

followed a guy in a plaid shirt into the woods. After a five minute walk, they came upon a crowd sitting around the perimeter of a hole the size of a basement. Above them, two wires were strung between the trees with battery-powered lanterns hanging from them. Tea lights rimmed the pit. Taylor opened a pint of whiskey and passed it to Dani as they sat with their legs hanging over the edge. There were probably 40 or so people, all in their 20s. A hearth dug deep into the far pit wall glowed hot with a fire and illuminated the face of a singer with a bushy beard and trucker hat, sitting on a camp stool and playing acoustic guitar, singing folk songs about how life is a difficult dance but still good. He sang with a country lilt, but not twangy, with themes of road life and relationships and loneliness.

Taylor leaned over to Dani and said, "He looks like he probably hasn't showered in weeks. I'd still fuck him."

Dani laughed and said, "Let's do it together."

The failed songwriter in Henry got jealous. He leaned back and listened to another song before he got up and walked into the forest. The music faded away with each tree he passed. From the top of a hill the city spread out in a grid of blinking lights. Considerable sprawl but not disgusting, then the open farms of the plains and the land he understood.

He looked across the Front Range cities and towns for another second before he went back to find the girls leaning into each other, blissed out. He sat with them. Dani passed him a joint and he was drawn into the music and the scenery and reconnected to the group. What a life to be so unconcerned with anything but the moment, he thought. He hoped he could remember how important it was to stay as present as possible.

On the drive down from the forest, he sat in the back and let the scenery roll by without any traction, a blur of treetops through the window.

In the morning he woke up not wanting to talk to anyone, wishing he was in his own apartment, or at least in a place where his roommates weren't friends and lovers. They walked around upstairs, showered, ate breakfast, got ready for work. The introvert in him said stay under the covers. He checked Craigslist and found something that looked suitable.

Out of politeness, he put on shorts and a T-shirt and went up before they left. Taylor stood with her back against the counter, sipping coffee and checking her phone. Dani was at the table peeling an orange.

"I think I found a place," Henry said. "Should be moving out soon."

"You just got here," Taylor said.

"I know. We'll still see each other."

"We'd better," Dani said. "Don't forget about that job offer."

5.

The building sign flickered in cursive pink neon: CAL's. Danielle walked up to the doorman and slid her ID out of her wallet. He handed it back without a glance and stared out at the street. She sat at the bar and ordered a whiskey and ginger. The bartender turned sideways as she mixed a drink in a cocktail shaker, pumping her toned arms, the ice rattling loud enough to echo across the room.

Malice danced on the main stage with her blonde and black Mohawk spiked up and proud, the sides of her head shaved and dyed in leopard spots. Heavy makeup on. She moved to Nine Inch Nails' "Closer" with enough anger to keep the beat. Her body was lean—a tired cat with a distant and hollow gaze. She spun and hung upside down and held herself horizontal on the pole—a range of skillful dance techniques requiring effort and concentration, even though her eyes were dull and bored. She lay on her back, her feet up and legs pressed together in black leather boots. She opened and slammed them together again, *thwack, thwack, thwack*, then she rolled on her side and crawled away on all fours, giving a backward glance to the people in the audience. Danielle wondered if she had a chance with her. Then she made fun of herself. Yeah sure you probably do. You're different from everyone else in here. You're special.

The next round of girls came out, each one with a slightly different style and routine. The moves were similar but done in a different rhythm and combination. In a way, Danielle admired these women, using their youth and beauty as currency. It must be empowering to be so bold, she thought. She also recognized the job was hard and sad, and she doubted they were treated well by the patrons or the management. No benefits and no one wanted to tip in this economy. After two more songs, she was about halfway through her drink when Malice came out in a black hooded sweatshirt and stood by the DJ booth at the end of the bar.

Dani finished her cocktail in one drink, her cheeks puffing out before she swallowed. She slammed the glass down and went over to Malice and tapped her on the shoulder. Malice flinched then turned to her.

"Hi, sorry," Dani said. "I just wanted to let you know I thought you killed it."

"Heyyyy," she said, guarded, with her towel in one hand and a questioning look.

"You can tell me to fuck off," Dani said. "Or you can string me along and pretend you like me so I spend more money. I wouldn't be mad at that. This is your job. I respect it. I also imagine management frowns on you interacting too much with customers."

"Hey, Tom, I'm taking a break," Malice said to the bartender then glanced at Danielle and went out through the front and into the night air. They stood by the parking lot. The neon sign hummed behind them. Malice lit a cigarette.

"You look like the kind of girl who has a girlfriend," Malice said, plucking a flake of tobacco from the tip of her tongue. "Or a boyfriend."

"What's that mean?"

"Nothing. You just look ... normal. Latina, right?"

Danielle narrowed her eyes, a challenge.

"Sorry. I like to ask," Malice said. "You could be indigenous, or Samoan. Who knows? How's your Spanish?"

"*Mal.* I rebelled against all that shit as a kid. Thought it was dumb."

Danielle watched her lips circle around the tip of her cigarette.

"I have to go back in."

"Wait. What's your real name?"

"I never give that out." She paused for a second then said, "Flannery."

"Like O'Connor?"

"Who's that? Should I know?"

"Some dead writer from the South. We had to read her in English class."

Flannery stabbed her smoke into the ashtray on the high-top.

"What's your number?" Danielle asked.

Flannery laughed. "Let me see your phone."

Danielle gave it to her. She called her right there so she would know if the number was real. It was. She watched as Flannery saved her name into her phone.

"This is really happening," Dani said.

"It is. Call me."

Dani thought about going back in, but decided she'd done all she should. The Uber ride back to her house was a blur of excitement.

When she got home Taylor was asleep in the bed. She went to the backyard with the dogs and lit a blunt, the city noisy and warm and alive around her, full of possibilities, temptations and ways to ruin a life.

Downstairs, Henry was sitting at the work table writing. He heard Danielle come home, but was feeling too locked in to get up and talk. He wanted to imagine what Danielle and Taylor felt when they came to the city. He wrote:

Drive into this city from the east and the north. Two seekers in a car looking for the dark peaks. Young creatures with no form. Into this city on land more plains than mountains. More midwest than west. Into the middle of the neighborhoods where decades ago the jazz horns blew all night, and now the dance music sparks in the wires overhead. Seeking. Seeking to walk these streets canopied by trees, past mansions of history lost to time and never to be told, graveyards now haunted parks, the sidewalks paved over bones. To leave behind all that sad open land, the lonesome landscape, for even more isolation among the crowds who come anew with the same rented trucks and the same dreams. Rural refugees washing up on the shores after crossing an ocean of grass.

They gaze at the two peaks, mountains that ages before the car and the town and the city, before these white people, guided tribes home. It'll be years before these two know the names the white people gave them and they'll never know their first names. Only that they're west of the city and rising above the ridgeline they won't see unless they stand on rooftops or climb trees. They've forgotten how to climb trees. And where is all the water? Where are the lakes? The rivers? One flat stream trickles through the city in a foreboding toxic run no one braves unboated.

Hope from the bars and the first jobs and the first friends. Each choice, each yes, closes off all others behind and splinters into a cracked web of paths ahead.

So much freedom. So little money.

At least the city feels welcoming. The skies are iridescent blue in the afternoon, the sun there for the taking. If only the stars would shine their lights, too, then they might know the way back home. But the two of them made a vow to each other. They're never going home, no matter what happens. Home is now the journey, and the trip goes on until it's over. So keep going until the city devours them.

6.

The apartment Henry decided on was a one-bedroom in a hundred-year-old, U-shaped brick building that surrounded a cobblestone-paved courtyard. His place was partially furnished with a futon bed and metal table with two chairs. There were hardwood floors, a gas stove and oven and a bathroom with a tub and shower. Shared laundry in the basement. The windows faced west and let in afternoon light.

Before he looked for more furniture he took an Uber out to Aurora, where a guy was selling a green 1970s Schwinn road bike off of Craigslist. The frame was scratched up and the decals peeling off—in bad enough cosmetic shape to keep thieves away. It felt solid—the gears all shifted smoothly. For $75 it was a good enough deal. He rode back through the city in the bike lane where he could, and where he couldn't he gripped the handlebars white-knuckled on the streets, intimidated by pickups. At least now he had a form of transportation better than walking and cheaper than the bus or rideshare apps.

He had gotten around by bike in other cities he'd lived in, and it was a good way to get to know a place. He felt a sense of self-reliance in his ability to travel the city under his own power. He was also worried he would run out of money, and buying a car would only make that happen quicker.

He carried the bike up the steps to his apartment and leaned it against the wall. The place was quiet, lonely. After he drank a beer checking his social feeds, he went to a bar around the corner with a flyer on the door reading Denver's All Inclusive, All Are Welcome Bar. A chalkboard above the bar said Tuesday night was bears night, and not the Chicago kind, Wednesday night was a post-party for the local women's roller derby team and Thursday a David Bowie-themed music night. He sat at the bar and ordered a burger and an IPA. The bartender was nice—a big, Midwestern-type guy with a soft, high-pitched voice—and Henry ate slowly, happy for the entertainment, careful not to run up the bill.

In the morning, when he took a shower he noticed his lower abdomen was dotted with pustules. Red, zit-like sores. About 30 spots between his belly button and pubic hair. They weren't painful unless he tried to squeeze them, but they wouldn't pop.

He went on-line and self-diagnosed the problem, ruling out herpes or something equally troubling. According to his rapid googling he appeared to have molluscum. He figured he had somehow picked it up in his travels and it just showed up now. Apparently it was a highly contagious skin disease, often sexually transmitted. He told himself he probably got it from a hostel. As much as he was trying to avoid it, he was in danger of turning into a character from a Bukowski story.

He remembered the Planned Parenthood directly across the street from Taylor and Danielle's house. He called and made an appointment for that afternoon, when the women would be at work so there was no chance they would see him, and rode his bike down to their neighborhood. It was a nice ride, slightly downhill, and on bike paths most of the way. The bumps itched under his belt as he rode.

He locked his bike on the sidewalk rack and passed a protester holding a poster with a graphic picture of a dead baby. Inside, he checked in with a gruff older man and sat with the pregnant women and the scared girls and a lot of other depressed people without health insurance who were scrolling on their phones.

When it was his turn, the young female doctor evaluated him in the patient room and confirmed his self-diagnosis. She said, "You can wait. It'll probably clear up in a few months. We can burn them off with liquid nitrogen if you're sexually active, or if you're changing partners. Otherwise it won't harm you at all. You have a strong immune system to have it so well-contained, so you'll probably be fine if you wait."

He grabbed a handful of free condoms from the bowl on the counter and rode his bike back home. This was the most concerning development to happen in his life in some time. What if he did want a new partner? He definitely did want to have some fun, though "partner" might be pushing it. He didn't have health insurance. He decided to wait. If they didn't go away he'd get them burned off.

He rode down to the 16th Street Mall and went to Target for basic necessities—shampoo, toothpaste, antacids, painkillers. He expected the experience to be comforting, easy, but when he walked in all he could hear was the noise of too many choices. This is what his friends in Asia who had come home then went back had warned him about. He stood in front of a rack of 50 different types of toothpaste—whitening, fluoride, sensitive, 3-D. *3-D?* He picked a decent brand for a slightly discounted price and tossed it in his red basket. On to the shampoo, and again, dry scalp, 2-in-1 with conditioner, silky smooth, for men. He bought the generic version of a well-known brand and saved himself $1.29. He walked away with the bottles calling to him.

He scanned the items through the self-checkout kiosk, and left the store, the chattering products cut silent when the automatic doors whooshed shut.

When he got back from the store he asked himself, *If you were a tourist in this town with only a few days to explore what would you do? Visit the mountains? Go hiking? Check out a dispensary? Yes. All of these.* If he was just visiting he would have gone straight from the airport to the nearest pot shop for the novelty. So that's what he decided to do.

It was early—his sleeping schedule not fully adjusted to this time zone yet—and he drank sencha tea and ate clementines in his room, checking social media and email until the marijuana store closest to him opened.

When the time came, he rode north in the warm midday air, the oak and maple trees arcing into a canopy overhead, past the large homes separated into apartments. Where once a family of five lived now there were four one-bedrooms. He had the eyes of a traveler and looked for beauty where he could find it—in the Victorian brickwork architecture, in the clouds curling over the city.

What about the people of Denver? Let him try to explain it as a journalist who wanted to be a culture critic might. His neighborhood had a lot of hipsters. The simplest, easy description. But, if asked, he would have struggled to succinctly describe the fashion or the culture of the strangers he passed on the sidewalk. The people he passed represented some form of subculture—be it the aging punk in tall leather boots and all black, or the finance-type in a plaid button-down under a fleece Patagonia vest, or the yoga class attendee's skin-tight leggings, mat slung over one shoulder. Skinny jeans on cyclists. Mohawked motorcycle riders. No one, single, defining culture. Far too much attempted individualism. Attempted individualism was the culture.

Then there were the people who lived on the street. For these people a lifestyle, a personal brand, a fashion aesthetic wasn't a priority, or even possible. They weren't influencers. They slept in the margins, in the spaces between buildings, under blankets and sleeping bags, sheltered by a pilfered shopping cart piled high with clothes and food and the day's dumpster finds. He avoided trying to explain away what he saw—he was reminded that if this was Indonesia, or Mongolia, or anywhere else he had traveled, he wouldn't be making judgments about the people on the street, he wouldn't blame the individuals, but he would make a judgment about the country itself and how it took care of its people. In the countries he had visited, few trusted their government in that way. It was the populace's duty to care for the sick and addicted and mentally unwell. By the dozens of people he witnessed sleeping in the alleys next to dumpsters, it was obvious Americans were doing a poor job of caring for their own.

He sniffed out the dispensary. The pine and skunk odor of raw cannabis came from a block away. Sugar Magnolia—Taylor and Danielle's company. The next marker tipping him off: the security guard with a gun on his belt standing next to the door. He locked his bike to a street sign and went in. His driver's license had expired years ago, but carrying his passport made him feel like he was still traveling. He slid the blue book under the glass window with a piece of paper taped to it advertising: Budtenders wanted. Minimum wage plus tips to start. Opportunities for advancement.

The receptionist handed the passport back with a number to be called. As he waited, he tried to work out what he thought about marijuana.

He had first smoked it in high school. He was one of a few in his group of friends to try it. He and his friend Jason were at a party, more of a small gathering in a basement, someone's parents were out of town, and Mark, this skinny, long-haired, brunette boy, had a joint. Henry and Jason hung back to see what happened to the other guys when they smoked it. As with most substances ingested by boys that age—high-caffeine soda, chewing tobacco—it made them more wild for a while. They said stuff that didn't make sense and laughed and laughed. One guy turned on loud, guitar-heavy rock, Rage Against the Machine, then Tool, and they really got into the music. Headbanging. Screaming. Knocking furniture over.

When the other boys tired out and found the pure pleasure of playing video games while high, Mark came over and sat on the floor in front of Jason and Henry. The skin on

Mark's face was dry and pinkish from his acne medication—cracked lips peeled back over his braces. And for all of those teenage imperfections, his red eyes burned with an energy and purity of life.

"We're getting pretty weird," Mark said. "I don't want you to feel left out."

"You guys are always weird," Jason said.

"So. What's it like?" Henry asked.

"Funny you should ask." Mark kept his smile as he reached in the front pocket of his hooded sweatshirt and produced a slightly bent, thin joint. He gave Henry the lighter. "Try to hold it in."

Jason laughed and said, "Fuck that." Henry saw this as a way to prove his bravery. He took the joint and lit it. He had only smoked a few cigarettes, hated those, and he wasn't sure he was going to properly inhale. But he didn't want to come off as weak. He pulled until smoke filled his lungs. He coughed and coughed then spat. Mark put his arms up and said, "All right!"

"Is it going to do that to me?" Jason asked.

"One more," Henry said, hoping to do it better the second time. On the second hit he tasted the pot, which reminded him of how the country smelled in the spring when the farmers burned the weeds in the ditches. Jason stared at Henry and Henry stared at the video game on the TV. Mark could see him getting sucked into it, and being a good shepherd of the first-timer he wanted to make sure Henry's experience went well. "Let's go outside," Mark said.

They went to the backyard, bundled up in heavy coats and gloves, looking up at the three-star belt of Orion. Mark and Henry laid down in the snow. Jason wouldn't come out in the yard, instead standing by the house. "Is this all we're doing?" he asked. "Fucking stargazing?" Mark jumped up and went to him. "Come over here," he said, and lit the rest. Jason took the joint from him without smiling and turned away when he hit it. He coughed, too.

They were lying there in the snow, watching for shooting stars and satellites. Jason kept saying he didn't feel anything. Then he said, "Guys, I can't see past my nose. No, seriously. It's really in the way," and they couldn't stop laughing.

The receptionist called Henry's number and the door buzzed as it unlocked and he was back in the dispensary. He walked into a room of bright, clear light and a U-shaped counter. A woman with dyed silver and blue hair greeted him from behind the sparkling glass case.

"I'm going to have a lot of questions," Henry said. "Dispensary virgin."

"Welcome then. Do you know what you're looking for in terms of experience?"

"I mean, I want to enjoy my day? Not get too ripped."

"Do you want to relax, or feel energized, or focus on something?"

"Not really looking to relax. I'd rather not get so stoned I can't move."

"Sounds like a sativa strain, not an indica. The way to remember the difference—indicas are more of a body high, more for sleep. Indica—in da couch. Sativas are more for energy and creative projects. We also sell hybrids in our flower, oils, and concentrates."

"Sativa then. What are my options for formats, for lack of a better word?"

"We have several different form factors."

"That's what I meant."

"For discreet and easy, your best option is probably a vape pen. We have disposable pens with 100 milligrams of THC, or 50/50 THC and CBD. THC gets you high. CBD is more for relaxation. Or we have vaporizers. You buy the battery and cartridge separately. Those come in a lot of different combinations. Some only vaporize oil, but others vaporize oil, flower and bud, and concentrates."

"What are concentrates?"

"Concentrated forms of marijuana, sometimes up to a hundred percent THC."

"Is that dabbing?"

"Right. So for that you have a bunch of options as well—shatter, wax, budder, live resin, rosin, terp sauce, terp diamonds."

She tapped her fingernails across the glass with one quick roll.

"Seems a little too advanced for me. What about edibles?"

"We have a full range of edible marijuana products. I like to caution any first-timer with these, especially if they don't have much of a THC tolerance. People consuming more marijuana than they can handle happens a lot. They get too impatient. The edible isn't kicking in so they decide to take another. It can take more than an hour depending on how large you are, whether you just ate, a bunch of different reasons. We always say start low, go slow. Start with five milligrams of THC and go up from there."

Henry scanned the products again. He'd already forgotten half of what she told him.

"It can be overwhelming your first time. Take as long as you need."

Despite what she said, as soon as it went quiet he felt pressured to buy something. Other customers waited in the lobby. He bought a disposable vape pen with a sativa-hybrid hash oil, a pre-roll of an indica-hybrid strain called Peter's Cologne, and a box of chocolate-covered coffee beans with 5 milligrams of THC and 5 milligrams of CBD. It cost about $80 with tax. He hoped it would last him a while.

Henry walked out with a stapled paper bag and opened it on the sidewalk. The vape pen was the size of a BIC ballpoint and when he drew on it the tip glowed green. Lemons and petroleum filled his mouth. He got back on his bike. In minutes, the cannabis was working, narrowing his eyes and opening up his senses. The city music came on heavier.

He was more receptive to how simply riding down the street gave his life drama. He started to fixate on a moment from his past—a conversation with his mother where he said something he regretted that couldn't be resolved. He had forgotten potent weed could do this to him, surface old anxieties and insecurities. Luckily he carried his headphones.

He was almost 30 years old riding the streets of a new city, high, with the hopes and prospects of young life. He felt invincible. He was young. He wanted to keep it going.

7.

<hr>

The Lyft dropped Danielle off at the end of an alley in a neighborhood east of downtown. She went down a set of stairs to a place calling itself a speakeasy, but it was just a normal spot with old-fashioned cocktails. She went in and sat at the bar. A projection screen TV at the end of the room played UFC videos. Men in tight shorts and fingerless gloves wrestled and punched each other in an octagon ring. A lot of women considered the fights to be silly, but she'd grown up with them, the men in her family getting together in front of TVs at homes or in bars on the weekends, so she didn't mind. To her they were always there.

The place was quiet, but low, heavy, rock music filled in for background noise. The short bartender wore his dark red trucker hat backwards and he looked like he ordered the rest of his outfit—white and blue plaid shirt, suspenders, jeans and boots—out of a lumbersexual catalog. She ordered an old fashioned with a splash of Grand Marnier. The bartender sprinkled bitters into a cocktail shaker with ice. A man with a beard, glasses, and a bald head sat on the opposite end playing the Megatouch machine. A couple of college students argued over their phones. Across an empty stool from her a dark-haired girl in a black tank top with tattoo sleeves sipped on brown liquid over ice.

"I can't believe how hot it got," Flannery said, putting her hand on Dani's shoulder as she sat down. "I wish I had some place to go swimming. I miss L.A. What are you drinking?"

"Whiskey."

A pause.

"'Whiskey.' Big on conversation are we?"

"Sorry. This old fashioned is made with a 10-year bottled-in-bond bourbon with notes of caramel and cherries and dark chocolate."

"Now you're being a nerd."

"Do you want to taste it?"

"Not that. Wine. Something cold. Can you order it for me? I'm going to use the bathroom."

Danielle watched her walk away. She thought of people as new places. How new romances were getting on a plane to a place she knew nothing about. She'd seen this woman work and had been seduced and wanted to know if she could take this somewhere real. She told herself she wasn't falling in love. She had talked to a girl and they were into each other. That's it. All they were doing was talking, anyway. She hadn't convinced herself of any of this.

"So you're a business woman?" Flannery asked as she sat back down. "A boss bitch?"

"I learned a long time ago I can't really work for other people."

"That's badass. I want to do that."

"It was a massive grind getting it started, but it's starting to pay off. If we don't fuck up and end up in jail."

"Why would you end up in jail?"

"Oh that's a long story. I'll tell you about it some time." Danielle looked around. "Can I ask you a personal question?"

"Why dancing?"

Danielle nodded.

"So boring. But OK. I'm trying to save up enough money for community college. Nursing school. And I didn't really want to wait tables or do sales. I mean, that's all trying to charm people out of their money, too. Dancing seemed more honest. Plus, it's fun some of the time. When the money's good and the customers aren't creeps."

"That has to be the most terrifying thing in the world, to be naked in front of drunk strangers."

"You get over it. That's what the money's for."

She smiled at Danielle and looked older than she was.

"Why is this place so dead?" Flannery said. "By Prohibition-era, did they mean that this place prohibited anything interesting from happening?"

"They're prohibiting people from getting laid, that's for sure."

"You want to see something? I used to work in a restaurant over here. I know this block." Flannery got up and Danielle followed her out to the street. She led them into a residential building two doors down. They went in the side entrance, up several flights of stairs and out onto a rooftop. From there they could look out over the neighborhood and across to the city skyline, the cash register-shaped building, and the rising foothills, the distant mountains outlined in blue. Beyond them a deeper layer of blackness, then the pale sky and a yellow half moon and the few stars burning bright enough to shine through the city light. They stood a few feet apart, making comments about how this place was not what people thought it was, how the mountains were not that close, how they could be anywhere in the Midwest as much as they were in the West. It was the perfect place to lean in and make a simple, innocent move. It all meant nothing yet.

8.

———————————

"Louie! Stop!" Taylor said, half laughing but slightly annoyed. He was on the bed wheezing, jumping back and forth between the two women—his breath terrible.

"Get your dog," Danielle said, laughing.

Taylor rolled off Danielle and kicked at the comforter. Louie jumped on her chest and tried to give her a kiss. "Gross. Off!" The dog only got more animated. "I guess we're done."

"No, wait. My turn." Danielle went under the covers and Taylor set Louie down off the bed. She tried to ignore his whining and panting. Danielle stayed down until Taylor squeezed her legs together and tapped her on the head.

Danielle came up and lay her head down on the pillows. Louie ran around to her side. "Aye, perro," she said. "Good morning, you filthy animal."

Taylor went into the bathroom and brushed her teeth as she let the shower get hot. For the moment, she wasn't thinking about the cops or the van or the weed they lost.

She dressed in jeans, ankle boots, and a white, v-necked T-shirt. As she put on her shoes Danielle said, "I'm just going like this, hope that's all right." She was wearing dark gray leggings and a light-blue, button-down shirt and her hair was up.

"You look good to me," Taylor said. "You always look good."

They walked a few blocks down to the restaurant specializing in tiny donuts. The sun in the east had cleared the treetops and it was bright and the birds were out. The line for breakfast wasn't terrible yet, so they stood on the corner looking at their phones as cars passed before the hostess called Taylor's name.

Their server, a tall man with a handlebar mustache and a turquoise green vest, took their order with a tone that failed to mask his contempt. They both knew, because they had worked these jobs, that the general consensus among the service industry was only real assholes went to brunch. The food was cheaper than at dinner so the servers, hungover and unhappy about working on a weekend morning, got smaller tips. Often, the customers were hungry and uncaffeinated and grumpy about having to wait in line for breakfast, so the whole situation started off poorly. But Taylor also took pride in tipping well, so she figured it evened out. They both ordered coffee and Danielle the salmon eggs benedict. Taylor asked for blueberry pancakes and a side of bacon.

While they waited, Taylor listened to the couple next to them. The guy, bearded, with glasses and a T-shirt with a picture of a band Taylor hadn't heard of, was reading from his phone, telling the woman across from him about an email he had received. "Pre-sale starts at 10 a.m.," the guy said. "First round of tickets get in the GA section down by the stage. I've never been that close at Red Rocks." The woman, also in glasses with curly, light brown hair, said, "Let's do it. That last show was so windy we could barely hear the music from where we were sitting."

"Oh fuck," Danielle said, swiping at her phone.

"What?"

"Wesley just texted. Apparently the cash is wrong at the downtown store."

"Don't say 'oh fuck' like that. I thought the cops called or something. My phone's almost dead. The cash is wrong how?"

"Either someone screwed up the count or they stole it. They don't have enough. He's going to check it out."

Taylor took a sip of her coffee and the bitter flavor set her mood right.

"Let's try not to talk about work today," Danielle said.

"Agreed."

Their food came on big white plates, and despite his surly attitude, Handlebars refilled their coffee when they needed it.

"Shouldn't we be taking advantage of the bottomless mimosa special?" Danielle asked. "Sunday Funday?"

"I thought we wanted to be somewhat productive today."

"Did I say that?" Danielle said. "If I did I didn't mean it."

When Handlebars came with the check Danielle said, "Actually we'll do a pitcher of grapefruit mimosas."

"Finally. I thought you two would never order real drinks," he said.

The food they couldn't finish they put in a box for the dogs and would later leave behind on the table. One glass of cheap champagne and grapefruit juice in Danielle said, "So I need to tell you about something." She took the sweating mimosa carafe by the neck and poured another drink.

"I'm listening."

"I have a crush on one of the girls at Cal's."

"Of course you do. Which one?"

"Malice. Her real name's Flannery."

"You know her real name. Wow. It is serious." She sat back in her chair and put her fingertips on the base of her glass.

"Not at all," Danielle said, her face slightly flushed. "But I think she might like me back."

"She might *like you back*? Are we in high school? First you have a crush, and now she might like you?" Taylor let out a tough laugh.

Danielle drank from her flute and filled it back up. "Why are you being so judgmental? Are you mad?"

"Of course not. Do you think it's going to go anywhere?" It was Taylor's turn to fill up her glass.

"It might go somewhere, but maybe not where I want it to go."

"Which would be?"

"I don't know. It just seems like it could be something fun."

"Are you that bored? Am I that boring?"

"That's not what I meant. You really don't like this, do you?"

"I'm not saying that. I'm also finding it … interesting." Taylor took a sip. "This is another one of your conquests, isn't it? Like Jamie and Brie and, who was the one in college … Tracy?"

"It's nothing yet. A crush. That's all."

"Well, I'm talking to two guys on Hinge. You're doing real life drama. I can't wait to see how this goes. Maybe I am just jealous." She picked up her phone.

"Oh fuck. For real this time."

"What?"

Taylor scrolled up and down on her phone. Her mouth drawn downward as she sat back in her chair. She tapped at her phone a couple more times before she showed Danielle. "Henry just texted us this."

The link went to a website story from the local TV station in the town closest to where they'd ditched the van. First posted on the Nebraska Crime Stoppers Facebook page, the article wasn't much. Essentially a repurposed police report looking for the owners of a van abandoned in a cornfield, with a small reward for any information.

"You know what we could do?" Danielle said. "We could call that anonymous tip line and tell them who used to own it."

"If they track those idiots down they'll say we stole it. No. We can't do shit."

"What if we at least call in a fake story? Waste their time?"

"When did you tell Henry about this?"

"The other night when we were all out."

When the carafe of champagne was gone they got their check. Danielle pulled up Uber and called a car as they gathered their belongings.

"Andre's three minutes away in a black Camry," Danielle said. "4.8 stars. Good reviews for his 'conversation.'"

"Oh Jesus," Taylor said.

They left Handlebars a 25 percent tip and Taylor wrote Thanks for taking care of us :) under her signature. She stood up, woozy, unbalanced, warm.

They put on their sunglasses the second they stepped outside. They walked to the corner and watched for the black car to come to a stop. Taylor opened the door for Danielle and slid in behind her.

Andre said, "How we doing this morning? Afternoon?" He talked to them in the rearview mirror. "Bottled water and mints in the seatback pockets if you care for them."

Danielle and Taylor both pulled up their phones.

"Headed to the Wide Receiver. That's new, right? Just opened?"

"Denver's first gay sports bar, whatever that means," Taylor said.

They drove on Colfax toward downtown. "Shoot, I don't like sports much either," Andre said. "Opiate of the masses. No time for it. Probably better than sitting around smoking weed all the time. Probably better than sitting around watching sports *and* smoking weed."

"Weed's pretty terrible," Danielle said.

"Well now. People sitting around getting high all day when they could be out working, or whatever. But yeah, shit, I ain't never had to kick someone out of my car for being too high. Wake their asses up, maybe. Ask them to stop talking about weird shit? Definitely. They just want me to play their dumb music so they can enjoy the ride."

"My friend here was being a smart ass," Taylor said. "We own a cannabis company. We're big fans of the plant."

"That's what's up. You got any samples?"

"Not on us. You know we're running that program where Uber drivers can bring people to our stores for a discount."

"Ah, you're Sugar Magnolia, right?"

"That's us."

"Y'all are killing it. You really don't care how much weed I buy?"

"What do you mean?" Taylor asked.

"Shoot, maybe I wasn't supposed to talk about it."

"No," Taylor said. "What did you mean by that? We're always curious what people are saying about our stores."

"Nah, nothing. Just I heard Sugar Magnolia is the place to hit up if you need to buy a lot of chronic. Like *a lot* a lot."

"Have you tried that?" Danielle asked.

"Unh-uh. I'm not in that game. I'm legit. Straight. I've been down that road. I'm not trying to put my ass in jail."

Taylor gave Danielle a look.

"We're trying not to talk business," Danielle said. "It's our day off."

"Shoot, now that's a good plan," Andre said.

Out the window, the city scenery swept by easily. Taylor took a moment to appreciate it.

"All right. We're here. You two enjoy your day and if I ever get any customers who want to know where to get that good legal weed, I'll send them your way."

"Ah, you're a sweetheart," Taylor said.

Inside, the place could have been any sports bar in any other mid-level city. Flat screen TVs. Hightop tables and stools. A pool table and a couple of dartboards. The main difference was the clientele.

The place was full—exactly what they wanted. Something fun and comfortable and harmless.

"Even the fucking Uber driver is saying we're the place to buy a lot of weed?" Taylor said as they waited at the bar. She ordered a Greyhound and Danielle a tequila and soda.

"Strange for a guy who didn't seem like he was into pot to know that."

"We need to fix it."

"Or maybe lean into it?"

"We can't lean into it. We're already hot enough."

"We've been fine so far. Maybe this town really does want our tax dollars."

"I don't know. I'm still worried about the van. I don't want any extra attention."

They took seats at the end of a communal table. One guy—balding, hairy shoulders under a tank top—said, "Hey ladies. Just a warning. Whatever you do, don't drink our water. It might be a little too strong for you."

"Oh gay water is stronger?" Danielle said.

"I'm saying if you accidentally drink from the wrong water you might end up in a stranger's bed and you don't know how you got there and you can't find your pants."

"Don't threaten me with a good time," Taylor said.

"Seriously. What's so different about it?" Danielle asked.

"Not me, necessarily, but some of us don't want the calories from alcohol. So they dose their glasses. It's the gayest thing ever."

"So you're date-rape drugging yourselves," Danielle said. "Hardcore."

"All I'm saying is watch which glass is yours. Not that I would worry about someone dosing you. The guys around here probably think your face is cute but your vagina ... not so much."

"Good looking out," Danielle said, tipping her glass toward him.

"Yes, bitch. Shots on me. They make a yummy lemondrop."

As he went to the bar, Taylor raised her eyebrows and Danielle laughed.

"Before we get too drunk—are we okay?" Taylor asked. "I mean, is our business going to be okay?"

"No. I don't know. Maybe. I don't think so. I'm paranoid. Aren't you?"

"I'm fucking always paranoid. I can't stand it. I almost want to just turn myself in."

"I'm not doing that. No chance. They can catch us if they want us."

"Maybe I'm not built for this." Taylor looked sad.

"C'mon, you're built for this," Danielle said, smiling, trying to look brave. "We both are. We have to be. We're in it. And today? Today's perfect. Let's worry about tomorrow tomorrow."

When he came back they all took the sugary shots and the day started to slip away. Taylor and Danielle joined the group of guys, who talked about traveling and boyfriends and sex and the athletes on TV they found attractive. A sense of loose energy and inhibition crackled around the table. A few were already drunk, speaking profanely, alive, fun, desirous.

The afternoon picked up speed. Rounds of lemondrops and vodka drinks and soon it was dark. Danielle had a joint and they went out on the patio with two new friends and smoked it. This was about the time Taylor's memory lost traction and would only catch on some piece of action or conversation that was truly remarkable. She did not remember trying to talk to Danielle about Flannery. Though Danielle did. She remembered when they decided to go home and couldn't find their phones to call a car. They checked jacket pockets and purses and asked the guys to call them. Only to figure out they had both asked the bartender hours before if they could charge their phones behind the bar. Taylor never would recall exactly the last time she used her credit card.

When they got in the car they fell into each other in the

back seat of the Jeep SUV. The next day Taylor remembered how she fought to stay awake, to make sure they made it home. Danielle was out before they left downtown. Taylor stuck her head out the window and let the night air blow tears across her face. They stopped and got out and Danielle couldn't walk. Taylor woke up in the morning with all of her clothes on and no way to piece together all the moments they had lost. They would say the guys roofied them but they never did. They browned out all on their own accord.

9.

Taylor had a headache like someone was shredding her brain with two metal forks. She had barely made it to work on time in her business casual—gray slacks and a white button-down. She stood at the end of a conference table in front of a monitor with three words stacked in bold-faced type: Standard Operating Procedures. The problem, she was saying as she tried to breathe, was Sugar Magnolia's SOPs weren't detailed enough. She mentioned how in the past week three major incidents had occurred—all bad—and if the company wasn't in crisis mode yet it was getting there. She clicked to the next slide:

Major recent disasters:

1. Fire at the extraction lab. Did we cause it? Or did someone sabotage us?
2. Diversion of product on black market.
3. Sugar Magnolia's growing reputation as the place to buy multiple ounces in one day.

"These are all important, but the most concerning to me personally is the third. One and two are what everyone has to deal with. That last one's unique to us. Could be putting a target on our back."

Wesley Stone, the purchasing manager, walked in with a slanted smile. He was lean and tall, wearing his preferred attire—a plaid shirt, untucked, with dark gray chinos and desert boots. He sat down, squared his shoulders back and tilted his chin up. "What target on whose back?"

"We're getting to that," Taylor said. She drank from her tumbler of cold brew coffee, glancing at Danielle.

"I'd like to know what Wesley thinks," Danielle said.

Taylor gave her a quick look. Danielle's eyes were red around the edges. She had been 30 minutes late to work that morning, wasn't wearing any makeup and hadn't showered.

"Fine. Let's start at the top and work through these. What do we know about the fire?"

"That we shouldn't have hired Randy to manage it?" Danielle asked. "He was doing a great job, until, well, boom."

"Are we sure it was him? And not someone else?" Taylor asked.

"In my opinion, your problem is you're using butane," Wesley said. "It's the cheapest, right, and it's efficient. I get that. Until Randy or whoever thought he could smoke a cigarette next to the room with a highly flammable gas."

Taylor stared into the table then said to him directly, "We're all aware of what BHO's like." She turned to Danielle. "We need to be using the safety checklists. Protocols. Again, SOPs. Maybe increased security."

"I would say you need to be using CO_2," Wesley said.

"CO_2 machines cost like five hundred thousand dollars," Taylor said. "And can't process plant material as quickly."

"What's it going to cost to rebuild your lab? CO_2 is safer, creates a cleaner product, and once you have your machine configured you really only need to put the biomass in the chamber and push a button. Obviously it requires some maintenance, but it's not complicated to operate."

"I agree," Danielle said, looking at Wesley and quickly back to Taylor. "I mean, one clear solution would be to change equipment, right?"

"OK. Let's look at the financials and revisit this," Taylor said. "Maybe we could switch to solventless. People seem to want more of those products. Number two. A car with a trunkful of our product was stopped in South Dakota and now the regulators are watching us even closer. What do we think happened there?"

"Rogue employee?" Danielle said. "Someone really likes our shit?"

"What if someone did it on purpose?" Taylor said. "Bought a bunch of our stuff and didn't care if they got caught because they knew it would make us look bad to the regulators."

"We should keep going. But monitor it," Wesley said. "If we keep doing this my way we're going to make a lot of money."

"No obvious answers then?" Taylor said. "Get better employees and hope they don't steal is the best we can do?"

"The best thing we can do is to keep making money," Wesley said.

"I think we can do better, but let's move on to number three," Taylor said. "We're all over the city right now as the number one place to buy multiple ounces. It's on Reddit."

"That's a good thing," Wesley said. "Free publicity."

"We're not worried about our reputation?"

"I'm just happy we have one," Wesley said. "A lot of companies don't."

"I think we should consider making some changes," Taylor said. "You know if we fuck up our compliance we're screwed."

"I don't think we need to do anything different," Wesley said.

"Let's vote. Who's in favor of staying this course?" Taylor asked.

Two hands went up.

"Fine. For the record, this is a mistake. Let's just make sure we're staying compliant, keeping our cash secure."

"Are we having fun?" Danielle asked, half smirking, lightly tapping the end of her pen on the table.

Taylor looked confused.

"Because it seems like we're grinding," Danielle said.

"We just took the employees to an escape room and axe throwing," Taylor said. "We spent thousands of dollars. Morale's fine." She snapped her laptop shut and took another sip of coffee as the other two left the room. Back in the office with the door closed she said to herself in a mocking tone, "Are we having fun?" She leaned back in her chair and pulled up a dating app on her phone, one where the woman was supposed to make the first contact. She swiped through guy after guy until she saw one who looked alright—short blonde hair and good shoulders sitting on a beach in a tank top. He probably wouldn't care if one date never turned into two. Perfect. "Hey," she messaged. "I'm free tonight if you are. Happy hour?" She waited for a few minutes until he responded with "Yes! RiNo? Noble House? 5:30?"

She gave him three thumbs up and said, "See you there."

At home she dressed in American West chic—tan, ankle-high boots, tight, dark jeans, olive green vest over a cream-colored, lightweight top. She texted Danielle, who still wasn't home:

"Just got invited to drinks with Green Lantern. Could be a good vendor for us. Don't wait up."

She arrived at the brewery a few minutes late. The bar was crowded and a group was playing Risk on the table in the middle. She checked her phone as a bartender with strong thighs and pigtails poured the beer. A message read: "White shirt."

She took the beer and approached him. He pocketed his phone as he stood and gave her a one-armed hug. He smelled like black pepper and oranges. They sipped their beers and she tried to determine how exactly she was tricked by his profile, looking for the same angle he used for his picture.

"You're prettier in person," he said.

"That's a nice line. Sorry, but you don't look that much like your picture," she said. "Was it taken a long time ago?"

"I'm growing this for a fundraiser." He wiped at the mustache with his fingertips. "Some girls like it."

"Do they."

"Not that many, honestly."

"I think it makes you look old."

"Which some people are into."

"Do you drive a windowless van, too?"

He laughed and finished his beer. "I'm not going along with that joke."

"I wouldn't. I would shave it off." Taylor looked at him in a serious way, but also with enough charm in her eyes to suggest more was possible.

"Advice noted. Can I get you another drink?"

He was tall, had a nice enough body, the kind of guy who would be happy with just a hookup. *What the hell, I made the trip.*

Later, in the dark of his apartment she was on top of him with her hands on his shoulders, trying not to think about work and Danielle but failing. He came. She didn't. She only paused for a second with her head next to his to catch her breath. He turned to her and said, "Thanks." She turned back to him and said, "That mustache makes you look kind of stupid."

Then she was in an Uber with the tall buildings of the downtown streets blurred in her side vision. The driver listened to EDM far too loud. He drove quickly, so she didn't complain.

At home, Danielle was asleep on the couch with a muted Austin City Limits concert on the TV lighting the otherwise dark room. Taylor got ready for bed and was almost asleep when Danielle came in and got under the covers.

"You smell like a dude," she said. "Hope it was fun."

"Shut up. I'm tired."

10.

Henry went to FedEx to print his resume then biked up to the brewery. The ad had mentioned serious heavy lifting, but when he got to the warehouse about half of the 40 or so people who were filling out applications were obviously physically unqualified, there just weren't that many jobs.

The two managers came in and sat at separate tables along the wall. They called for anyone ready to come up. Henry quickly stood and gave his resume to the warehouse manager—a guy in his 40s with a beard and a collared shirt with a name patch: MIKE.

"Have you ever driven a forklift?" Mike asked.

"No, but I grew up on a farm. I can operate a combine."

"How about manual labor?"

"I've been working in offices and classrooms for years. Manual labor sounds pretty good right now."

"Can you work fast?"

"I know how to work."

Mike marked the corner of the application.

"You just passed round one. Wait until your name is called."

He went back to his seat and in about 30 minutes the woman in charge of the restaurant, Jeannette, called him up.

"So guess what?" she said. "Two things: One, it's between you and another guy. He has more restaurant experience, but I think you're probably a better fit for the dock. Two, I like people from the country, and hiring for restaurant work is not an exact science. Can you start tomorrow?"

"I can."

"You need black jeans or pants and black shoes. We'll supply the shirts."

He thanked her without asking how much he'd be getting paid or what the hours would be. He would have worked 50 hours a week if they had wanted him to, or 10 hours a week and he would have looked for another job. His attitude was work led to more work, so he biked to Target and bought two pairs of black jeans and a pair of black, short-topped boots with non-skid soles that were ugly but functional.

The bike ride commute the next day took him about 30 minutes. Henry trained with a guy named Gary who had been a warehouseman for a number of years. Gary walked as though he had been lifting heavy things for a long time and gravity was starting to win. He shuffled stooped and stiff-backed. He wore a hat with the brewery's name on it and a collared shirt similar to Mike's, but instead his patch read DAVE. Henry asked him why he didn't have one that said GARY and he said, "Don't fucking ask." Henry watched as he stood on the loading dock and updated the keg inventory on a clipboard. Then they went over to the brewery and grabbed the empty kegs. Stacked them on pallets out in the yard. Gary had a way of talking where he wouldn't look Henry right in the eye, but just to the left or right of his head. Henry felt like there was someone standing over his shoulder. Gary also grunted most of the time.

"Hunnnnnh. I've gotta stop dating these Craigslist chicks," Gary said. "They're too fucking crazy for me. Hunnh."

Gary showed Henry how to kill time by sweeping the lot around the docks where the trucks came in, how to clean up the empty pallets, and how to clean the taps customers returned with their empty kegs. Running the forklift didn't take much to learn. Henry spent a few hours out in the parking lot spinning around, getting a feel for the brake and the steering, stacking pallets of empty kegs.

"One nice perk," Gary said. "Employee keg. Shift beers.".

The next day he was on his own, and when he came in he had the order for the restaurant written out by the closing bartender from last night's shift. He took the list and went down to the cooler and climbed the pallets of kegs stacked three high. He pulled an IPA barrel weighing about 160 pounds off the top pallet and dropped it onto a tire on the cement floor. He filled a pallet with six barrels then drove it over to the restaurant, getting as close as he could to the elevator. He grabbed the hand truck, slid a barrel onto it upright and secured it with a metal hook, then he rolled the second one over to the hand truck and deadlifted it sideways across the top of the upright keg. He wheeled them two at a time to the elevator and down to the restaurant's keg cooler in the basement, where they ran a dozen or more taps at the bar. That morning he loaded in 13 kegs.

The government's safety regulations stated any person carrying over 160 pounds was at risk for injury and should be assisted by another person. But doubling up wasn't the job and if Henry couldn't do it on his own they'd find someone who could. He took some pride in working with his hands and back to earn even a meager living.

On the day of his first shift working in the adjacent restaurant, Henry rode north through the city with a pale pink light on the horizon to the east, above that the sky fading lavender. The air was cool and it was good to be cycling through the city as it came alive. He arrived before the restaurant opened. He went down to the office and checked in with Jeannette. She handed him a clipboard with a checklist of tasks. He went upstairs and changed light bulbs, mopped the floor in the keg cooler, and stocked napkins by the hostess station. He was polishing the brass on the bar foot rail when one of the owners came in.

"Do you know where Jeannette is?" the bald, thin man

asked, not looking down at him, not bothering to introduce himself. Henry said she was downstairs and the man walked away without another word.

After the maintenance was finished Henry changed into a T-shirt advertising the brewery's beer. He wore a brown one with a yellow Volkswagen van on the front and a tall glass of hefeweizen on the back.

Henry moved fast around the restaurant, not the type to interact with the general public much.

Henry overheard John, the tall line cook, loudly proclaim from his station, "I don't trust a man who doesn't like football."

River, the young hostess with long black hair, who had all the kitchen guys chasing after her, was walking behind him as he carried a tray full of food and said, "I'm with someone, but we could make it happen. I won't say anything if you won't."

"What time do you get off?"

"Oh wow. I was sorta kidding," she said, and took another path through the tables.

A lot of would-be artists, fresh out of college, broke, riding bikes to work and spending all their money on rent to live with roommates.

That night he went back to his neighborhood on his own, tired but a pocket full of tip money. He stopped at a bar two blocks from his apartment. Inside, the light was dim, tinting the room yellow. Three men sat with exactly two stools each between them.

The place was ugly and smelled bad enough the hipsters wouldn't drink in it ironically. Henry was still wearing his work T-shirt and black jeans. He sat at the rail and ordered a Miller High Life and a shot of whiskey and watched the hunting show on TV.

Another old man in a worn, gray T-shirt that said Daytona Beach Motorcycle Rally and a cowboy hat sat at the curve in the bar next to a guy with white, thick lamb chops and a blue western shirt with pearl snaps. The first one set his hat on the bar and the bartender tossed over a coaster and poured him a pint of Coors. When the beer came he quickly signed, "Thanks" and made a sound almost like a word. The man next to him did not seem to care that they wouldn't be having a conversation.

Henry took another shot then left and rode over to the forested cemetery with graves of Europeans and Russians, Volga Germans. People who came to this land when it was mostly barren to grow sugar beets and raise cattle and drive out the natives. The stars were shrouded by wisps of clouds. Under the charcoal sky the black trees curled over the streets and the trunks groaned and popped. A rodent scurried ahead to take refuge in the trees. Henry continued in the wet grass with the woods all around him. He sat on a stone bench and listened. A shadow ran ahead of him. He recalled an Auden poem he had memorized. One of only a few. *O Where Are You Going?*

Did you see that shape in the twisted trees?

He wished he could see his own death. What a gift to know how you would die. If you live long enough, you go out hooked up to IVs in a hospital, hanging on though the outcome is certain. Prodded and poked by indifferent nurses, watching a television while your family stops by for a few hours here and there. No way to go.

The spot on your skin is a shocking disease

If he could make it to 60 that would be plenty.

From the edge of the cemetery, someone made a sound intended to be an animal but was clearly human. An attempt to be spooky, ominous. Pained cries. Tortured whimpers. A coyote with its leg caught in a trap. He walked toward the darkness until he came to a fence and looked into the woods. Nothing there but dark trees and the sky between them.

II.

———————————

Danielle and Taylor settled into their seats. They unfolded their napkins and sipped their waters. Staff in white shirts and black pants hustled across the floor. Danielle scanned the wine list then handed it to Taylor. The server, a man with a trim, gray beard and his hair slicked back in a ponytail, brought bread and olive oil, gave the specials, and took their order without writing any of it down.

In time, the server returned and noiselessly presented the bottle, rotating it to face the label and confirm the order. He deftly cut the foil wrapper off the top, spun in the wine key, soundlessly removed the cork, and poured a splash of the gigondas into Danielle's glass. She smelled it and nodded. He poured for each of them, twisting the bottle to keep it from dripping, left the cork on the table, and moved on.

"Here's to another store," Danielle said, holding up her glass.

Taylor lightly tapped hers against Danielle's and forced a smile. "Number five. Can you believe it?"

"You don't seem happy."

"No, I am. Really."

"OK, I'm not convinced."

"Aren't you worried a little bit?"

"About what?"

"About what? About going to jail?"

"I'm trying to put that shit behind me. We fucked up. What can we do about it now?"

"Nothing, I guess," Taylor said, tearing off a hunk of the baguette and dipping an edge in the green oil. She bit into the crusty bread and tasted the olives.

The food runner, a young woman with dark, thick-framed glasses and stringy, blonde hair combed to the side, delivered their plates over their left shoulders without asking who had ordered what. She silently combed the table for bread crumbs.

Danielle effortlessly cut off a piece of the lamb shank. She dabbed the meat into the horseradish sauce and took a bite, giving a quiet moan as she chewed.

Taylor took another sip of her wine. "I'm still thinking about Ben."

"We're all fucked," Danielle said. "We can't get rid of people. You can go on Instagram or fucking Google or whatever. That last girl, Winnie? I deleted her from all of the apps. Hadn't thought about her in months. Then one day I got an email suggestion from *LinkedIn* that we should connect. Fucking LinkedIn. Jesus Christ."

Taylor laughed. "One time I Googled an old girlfriend from years ago, not because I still had a thing for her, but because I was curious what happened to her life, and I found her fucking wedding registry. It was on the first page of results. Married to some dude in Ohio. I should've bought her a gift from Target. Fucking wine glasses. It's absurd." She wiped her fingertips on her napkin in her lap. "You look really nice, by the way. Is that a new top?"

Danielle's combination of makeup and her hair down on her shoulders and her exposed collarbones—it all made Taylor want to call a car and get a hotel room.

"No. I've had it forever."

"We need to do more of this," Taylor said, making circles with her hands. "Less work. More wine."

"We need to be paying ourselves better so we have the cash to do it."

"Yep, good point."

Danielle chewed, then she gave Taylor a look.

"What?" Taylor asked.

"I know we were talking about you, but I ran into Flannery again."

Their server came by and expertly filled their water glasses without touching them. He moved on without a sound.

"This is becoming a thing, isn't it?" Taylor asked.

"I think so. Fuck."

"I don't see the problem."

"The problem is shit like this usually doesn't end well."

Taylor's fish flaked with the slightest pressure from her fork. It tasted of tarragon and garlic and parmesan. "I'm jealous. Your drama's better than my drama."

"It's gonna be a mess."

"I love that feeling."

After creme brulee, they paid and walked across the street to a bar run by one of the old Greek families. A bald man in a suit at the door gave them each a white carnation. They took their flowers and ordered vodka tonics with lime. The place was loud and someone had loaded the jukebox with several dollars worth of soul music. They stood at a table and tried not to look around too much.

"I know I always say this," Taylor said. "But I love that we can talk to each other about anything. And I can handle whatever it is. Unless you go off and get married to some dude."

"Unless you go off and get married to some dude. That's more likely to happen with you than it is with me."

The night ended with them at the diner down the street, where the city's late-night people came together for omelets and hash browns and cheap coffee, slouching in the booth as their eggs got cold, comfortable and at peace with one another.

____

12

On the day of a planned company outing, Wesley walked past Taylor's office and she couldn't keep herself from laughing. He was wearing bright purple Nike sneakers and a white Adidas tracksuit with three purple stripes running down each arm. "Wes," she called out. "Come in here. I want to see your outfit."

"No such thing as too much in this industry, is there?" he said, straightening his collar and strutting down the hall.

"You look like an Eastern European gangster."

"Let's go watch some baseball."

As Wesley pulled away from headquarters, Taylor felt the cooled leather seats on the back of her knees. The car bothered her. Aside from her vintage motorcycle, Taylor drove the same CRV she had in college.

"How much is this outing costing us?" she asked. No one replied.

Wesley and Danielle chatted about the best way to get downtown as Danielle read aloud from the traffic report on Waze.

"I've been hitting this CBD cartridge all day," Danielle said, turning to the rest of the car and exhaling a plume of vapor. "I tweaked my knee at the gym. It's helping with the inflammation."

"Really? What cartridge are you using?" Taylor asked.

"We might want to do a promotion. People are always looking for CBD that actually works."

Danielle popped the cartridge out of the bottom.

"Oh, turns out I'm an idiot," she said. "This is actually a THC cartridge."

"You're so perma-high you can't tell the difference between THC and CBD?" Taylor asked.

"Might still want to promote it. It's doing the job." Danielle took another drag.

The staff mingled around the party deck at Coors Field, cocktails and beers in hand, all on the company tab. Taylor noticed Danielle sported expensive sunglasses she hadn't worn before, and Wesley was wearing a new watch that must've cost thousands of dollars.

Only minutes after the first tall beer she had to pee. In the bathroom handicapped stall next to her the shuffling of several pairs of feet, low whispers, and quick snorts. When the three girls went out to wash their hands and check their makeup they exploded into rapid-fire conversation. It wasn't that they were interrupting each other—they were all talking at once in a swirling torrent of words that followed some form of internal logic, quickly flowing from work at Sugar Magnolia to baseball to office gossip to weekend plans. Taylor waited for them to leave before coming out of her stall. To confront them at a work event would only make them skittish and ruin their day. No, she could tell by their voices who each of them were, and she made a note to send an email when she was back in the office, reminding them what they do at a company function reflected on the whole business. That they were representing the company when they weren't at work.

The work crew sat in the row of seats painted purple around the stadium designating the 5280-foot, one mile altitude mark. Past the scoreboard the sun slid into the mountains. Streaks of orange and gold smeared the sky. The weather was mild, but the quality of the sun and the light—

brilliant, painful without sunglasses—made their surroundings sharp and clear. She loved the strategy of baseball, how the pitcher and defense worked to control the eruption of violence brought on by the man with the bat. Nine against one guy with the potential to rip open the order of the moment and send them all scurrying into the far corners of the field to put a stop to the chaos. How time became a matter of precious seconds. How the skill and athleticism and success, or failure, of the team all depended on a small white piece of leather charged with the energy of these men in tight pants.

The pitcher went through his routine. He shook off the catcher's first two suggestions then nodded and gathered the ball into his glove. He wound up and hurled the ball faster than her eye could track, but she could follow the action, the crack of the bat and the hitter popping out but still jogging to first base. The centerfielder waved off the shortstop as he caught it and in one continuous movement threw it to the second baseman.

Midway through the third inning, most of the employees had abandoned their seats in favor of the party deck bar and some left the stadium altogether. Taylor hoped no one did anything dumber than what she'd already seen, like drive home drunk.

In the bottom of the eighth, with the Rockies well ahead, she looked around and she was the only one in their group still there watching the game. On the party deck, Wesley and Danielle stood with a circle of employees passing around a cannagar—a blunt wrap filled with premium flower, dipped in THC distillate, and rolled in kief—Wesley had given it to them when they opened their new store. It was burned down about halfway, with a bright red tip glowing like a lit-up cherry.

"Thanks for smoking without me," Taylor said.

"Oh shit. Pass that to Taylor," Danielle said.

A cultivation worker coughed as he handed it to her. The

soggy end had started to unravel.

"Gross," she said. "I'm going back to the office for a little bit. Last round of signing checks. I'll take a car."

"That can wait until tomorrow," Danielle said. "Enjoy yourself. We've got a room booked at the Ramble for the afterparty."

An eruption of noise from the crowd. Taylor would have to check the highlights on Twitter later.

13

"How dark is it?" Danielle asked.

Taylor leaned back and pointed across her body at Henry. He took a drink of his beer then left for the bathroom. As soon as he was out of earshot, Taylor said, "He's acting weird. Has barely said two words all night. No idea what's going on. Sit down. Get a drink."

Taylor's favorite dancer, Sunny, walked onstage to an old soul song by Etta James. She wore heavy eyeliner, her black hair unwashed and streaked with blonde highlights. She had several tattoos, but the most iconic was one of three stars across her hip bone, the stars progressively emptier as they moved toward her side. She was 21 years old and the main attraction. Taylor went up to the rack, folded five one dollar bills into a tent, and waited for Sunny to dance her way over and pick them up.

A guy at the other end of the room told the bartender there was a birthday in their group and Sunny brought the woman onstage, sat her in a chair facing the audience, and gave her a lap dance with the crowd watching, all while singing happy birthday in a low, relaxed voice. It seduced the woman so effectively they watched her go from a reluctant, blushing observer to a willing participant.

Sunny spoke into the microphone and addressed the crowd. "This beautiful goddess here is an old coworker of mine. She used to do some of this on her own. She won't dance anymore, but I'm going to dance with her."

They stood and swayed together as they gave an impassioned rendition of a Rolling Stones song. Before the song ended, a jealous boyfriend in a white hooded sweatshirt went up to his girlfriend or wife on stage and took her by the arm and led her out of the bar. They were fighting before the door slammed shut. Sunny yelled after them, "I love you!"

The song changed to a Prince tune, and Danielle flashed a half-smile, part embarrassed, part excited. Flannery came out in a leather jacket and knee-high fishnet stockings, a pink boa over her shoulders, her mohawk dyed pink to match. Danielle got up and went to the corner seat at the rack next to Taylor, who stood and said, "All yours."

Flannery wasn't looking into the crowd at the beginning of her routine. She focused more on her dancing, going through the moves. She watched Danielle as she shed her clothing.

Danielle wanted to tell Flannery about a car in the neighborhood. A restored convertible Thunderbird, pale blue with white upholstery and trim, for sale next to the diner Danielle ate at when she was hungover. Not far from where they were. She wanted to pick Flannery up in that car, tell her to pack her bag and they would head to New Orleans, or Nashville, or Savannah, or somewhere else warm and charming. Like some Bruce Springsteen song.

Danielle thought that Flannery was genuinely interested in her, flattered by her attention. She finished her two songs and went to the back. As soon as Danielle joined Henry and Taylor, they finished their drinks and said they were going home.

"Fine. Be lame," Danielle said. "I'm going to have another drink."

Danielle went to the bar and waited for Flannery to come out on the floor and troll for lap dance customers, but she sipped her whiskey until it was gone and she still hadn't shown up.

From the Uber, Danielle texted I waited for you but I'm going home.

Flannery responded, Sorry, girl, I was too tired. Went home. Call me tomorrow.

Get some rest. You were fire tonight. 🔥🔥🔥

When Danielle got home Taylor was sitting on a stool at the kitchen island drinking a can of grapefruit seltzer and looking at her phone. She glanced up, then went back to her phone.

"Told you this Flannery thing was going to be a mess," Danielle said. She went to the cabinet and took down a glass and filled it with filtered water from a plastic pitcher.

Taylor leaned toward her phone and with the other hand held out a half-smoked joint. "Kush, I think," she said.

Danielle lit it and leaned back against the kitchen cabinet. "Flannery's stringing me along."

"A stripper string someone along? Never." Taylor held out her hand to get the joint back. "We should set a boundary around some of this. Tell me when you hook up with someone. Don't tell me if they're irritating you. You sort that part out yourself. I don't want to deal with the drama."

"OK. Whatever you say."

Taylor set her phone down and grabbed Danielle's hand and they went to the living room. They turned on an old episode of a sitcom they used to like and fell asleep on opposite ends of the couch.

14.

Henry's first paycheck was depressing. Making minimum wage plus tips waiting tables 15 hours a week and $11 an hour hauling kegs on the weekends wasn't enough. He applied to a job ad to intern at the local alternative weekly newspaper. He had a day off in the middle of the week and they invited him to sit in on the editorial meeting. Fifteen minutes into the meeting it was obvious this was a bad idea. The staffers were unfriendly, protective, wanted to keep their jobs locked down. There were no paying staff jobs in journalism anywhere. A few places still had freelance budgets.

After the meeting, he sat at a computer in the corner of the office and wrote one blog post about a K-Pop band. They gave him the byline Henry "The Intern" Kaufman, so he left and never wrote for them again.

That night, Danielle and Taylor called him from the street. He went down and found they had brought over a small desk from their basement.

"How much do I owe you?" he asked.

"Just use it to write something good," Danielle said.

He carried it up and the first thing he wrote on it was a plan to freelance for all of the local outlets he could. He made a list of story ideas and compiled the email addresses of editors. He'd start pitching after work tomorrow.

When he got to work at the restaurant the next morning, Jeannette stood behind the hostess stand looking unhappy.

Word was River had come to work on ecstasy, started giving the other servers shoulder and back rubs and dipping her fingers into the beer cheese soup. She had asked one customer if she could pet his arm hair. Jeannette asked Henry to host customers, write down reservations, place the menus, and roll silverware, aside from his normal waiting duties. He flew through the restaurant, nearly running in the aisles, between the front door and the back room and the dish pit in the kitchen.

The night went by in a whirl of clearing empty beer mugs and twisting knives and forks into white napkins and, "Hi folks! How many tonight?" Then it was over and he was at the bar drinking his shift beer. Nebraska was playing baseball on TV, but he was the only one watching and he didn't care all that much. He walked out into the night to his bike locked to the No Parking sign. He wheeled the green Schwinn onto the dark street, rain pattering heavy in the puddles on the roof of the adjacent warehouse and the parked cars. He rode south, tires and wheels wet, soft lights white on the handlebars and blinking red under the seat.

Going downhill and at a good clip in the bike lane, he came up beside a gray Toyota Camry. It suddenly turned, trapping him so he had no choice but to lower his shoulder and slam into the front fender and side door.

The car stopped and an attractive, middle-aged lady stepped out. She was dressed up for dinner in a black dress and a silver necklace.

"Oh my god," she said. "Are you okay?"

He hadn't fallen over, but his wheel and handlebars were twisted.

"Hard to see in the rain?"

"I'm really sorry. You're sure you're OK?"

She gave him her business card and he rode home, his tire squeaking against the front fender. The bike wasn't permanently damaged, just needed straightening out.

Two days later he called her and asked if she'd like to grab a drink with him. He thought this was the perfect romantic opening. She said, "Oh honey, I've passed that time in my life. Go find yourself a nice girl your age."

15.

Wesley's laptop was plugged into a monitor at the end of the conference room. He called up a graphic charting their revenue. Expenses still far outpaced their total earnings, but their financials were trending in the right direction. The line graph showed a sharp rise not long after he was hired.

"This steady increase in revenue is great," Taylor said. "How are we explaining it? Word of mouth?"

"We've increased our advertising budget," Danielle suggested.

"And added several product lines, right?" Taylor was acting impatient. "What else?"

"That increase is largely the result of flower sales," Wesley said, looking down at the table. "We're moving pounds of bud out the door at a 100 percent-plus markup from the wholesale market price."

"And we attribute that sales volume to what?" Danielle asked.

"The sales initiatives we've put in place," Wesley answered.

"Meaning?" Danielle said.

"The program allowing repeated one-ounce sales. Let's continue down this path for a little while, and if you're not seeing the results you want we can re-evaluate. But for the time being I'd like to keep developing this program, and if we need to level-set and reassess at some point I'd be happy to."

"If it's working maybe we should keep going with it," Taylor said.

Danielle turned to Taylor and said, "If we're moving product and making money I'm good with it."

"Thanks for that vote of confidence," Wesley said. "Now let's talk about how we're going to keep our shelves stocked. Sales are only going to get better."

Taylor finished the day without doing any difficult, concentrated work, responding to emails and answering questions when people stopped by her office. She was Googling "white van marijuana Nebraska" when Danielle knocked on her door. "Happy hour?"

"Can't. Going for a ride."

Her search yielded no new results. She shut down her computer and took her bag to the bathroom to change into biking clothes.

The trailhead parking lot was moderately full for a summer weekday. She pumped air into the Stumpjumper's back tire, changed into her shoes and gloves, put on a helmet, and pushed straight up the steepest route. She usually saved the switchbacks for the way down, but today she wanted her lungs and legs to burn immediately. She wanted the release of strenuous exercise. To make her stop thinking about work and money and the van. She could coast back nice and gentle on the way down, after she got her head right.

When she made it up to the flatter section that wound around the side of the mountain she could move faster. Her bike raised dust on the dry trail. Pushing it as hard as she could took all of her focus. She thought only about the moves, the turns, the dangers and obstacles on the trail. She went west and looped through the steepest, most dynamic feature, making laps back up toward the radio tower. She was cruising now, in a flow state, only aware of the dips and the rises and the curves, the release she wanted.

Until a guy behind her dinged his bell and cleared his throat. *You can wait until we get to the junction.* But he was right behind her now. They were on a steep rise and it was slow going. He rang his bell again. *Oh fuck off dude. You can wait.* She pumped in low gear until the fork in the trail where she slowed to let him pass.

"Get out of the fucking way," he said, under his breath.

"What an asshole," she said, not really under her breath.

He went right, she went left. But the way the trails were designed on that part of the mountain they all ended up back in the same place. She made two more loops before heading down. She was coasting on the gradual stretch back to the parking lot when the same bell rang out.

"Why are you so slow?"

She hit the brakes and turned her bike sideways. The guy skidded, trying to stop, but had to take the brush to avoid hitting her. He hit his handlebars in a slow-motion, undignified crash that included some grunting. She laughed and waited to see if he was OK. He got up quickly so she went on.

Back at her car she changed out of her biking shoes and unstrapped her gloves. The guy's truck was in the spot directly behind hers.

"That move you pulled could've twisted my fork," he said.

"You pulled the move. I've been coming here for a while now and never had anyone act that rude."

"There's a lot of noobs out here. It gets annoying."

"The only noob I saw was the guy eating shit."

He opened up his bike rack and put down the tailgate. "Truce beer?"

"I'll drink a beer."

He tossed her a can. With his helmet off he looked normal.

"C'mon," she said, holding up the IPA. "Could you be any more of a cliché?"

"Hey, at least it's cold."

She took two sips. "This is horrible."

He laughed. "How often are you up here? I need a riding buddy."

"Probably not," she said. "I don't really have time for ... this. Whatever this would be. But thanks for asking."

She set her beer on his tailgate and drove off. She picked up some tacos from the market in their neighborhood and came home to Danielle with the lights low in the house. She sat on the floor by the couch and gave Dani her hand. Dani squeezed it and they watched old movies until it got late.

16.

Wesley stuck inspirational quotes on his computer monitor. They were written on yellow and pink Post-It notes and said things like "Hard work beats talent when talent doesn't work hard." And "PREVAIL." He called up an Excel spreadsheet with sales figures for the infused products the company carried, collated the products by sales from lowest to highest, and resolved to cut at least the worst 5% earners from the list. The receptionist, a guy in his 20s with dreadlocks who also worked on the packaging crew, brought his mail in and said, "Yo, 'sup, Wes?" but left when he didn't get a response.

Wesley sifted through bills and junk mail until he found one from the state's Marijuana Enforcement Division. The letter informed the owners of Sugar Magnolia they had been warned about the sales practices that allowed for "looping," or letting one customer buy an ounce, take it to a car in the parking lot, and return to the store for another. If they refused to comply with the law and stop allowing customers to "loop" the state and local authorities would take immediate legal action. Wesley reread the letter to commit it to memory, then stood and fed it into the paper shredder.

As he drove through the city the streets shimmered in the morning sun. He parked in front of Haviletsky's law office, a narrow business in a strip mall dominated by a pink, fake-adobe Mexican restaurant. On one side, a sandwich board outside of a brewery read, "All unattended children will be given energy drinks and taught to swear." On the other side, a clothing store offered discounted ski and snowboard gear on sidewalk racks. Except for the stenciled names of the partners on the glass door, there was no sign for the law office.

Inside, a young man sat behind the receptionist's desk typing at a keyboard. He said, "No solicitors. It says right there on the sign."

"I have an appointment," Wesley said.

"Then sit down."

Wesley sat on a cracked brown leather sofa and shuffled through a copy of a magazine—*Marijuana Industry Journal*. He peered at a full-page advertisement from Haviletsky and Pierce with the partners in suits, standing in a greenhouse, waist-deep in a sea of pot plants. They had dark sunglasses on and were both smoking a joint.

Haviletsky came out tucking his shirt into his pants, his gray hair combed straight back, and extended a warm hand to Wesley. "Welcome. Welcome. Step into my office," he said.

Wesley followed him back to a room with walls covered from floor to ceiling in plaques, certificates, and pictures of the lawyer standing next to people Wesley didn't recognize. As they sat across the desk from each other Haviletsky picked up a device the shape of a ballpoint pen, inhaled from it, and blew out a thin cloud of vapor.

"Already been a long day," he said. "Feel free to smoke whatever you brought with you. We're obviously pro-industry here."

"I'm good. Got a lot to do today."

Wesley explained what he wanted to do with the business. He outlined Sugar Magnolia's plans for expansion and, without going into great detail, conveyed how they would distinguish the business from the competition by marketing under a slightly more aggressive interpretation of the state's marijuana laws than the rest of the industry. He also told the lawyer about the letter. When Wesley finished, Haviletsky sat there, processing.

"Fascinating. Well, I certainly would want you for a client if that's how you're going to be operating your business. You'll need a good attorney. I can't tell you how to run your company. I'm not a consultant, but I will tell you this—you can find a gap to exploit by operating in a legal gray area and by relying on a literal interpretation of the language in the regulations. Or you can operate based on the spirit of the law, and not only do what seems right for you, but for everyone in the industry. Your choice. It's obviously a competitive market, and I could see how you would want an angle. If you choose this path you might not be crossing the line, but you're going to be driving right up to the edge of it."

"All I needed to hear."

"Like I said, I'd love to represent you going forward." Haviletsky leaned back and folded his hands across his stomach.

"Thanks. I'll call you if we need you."

"If this is how you're going to operate you'll need me. Remember this: Compliance is everything in this business. The regulators make examples out of people."

On his lunch hour, Wesley drove down to the animal shelter. He walked through the kennels with the penned-up dogs all eager for someone to help them escape. He wasn't exactly sure what he wanted, or if he even could take care of one properly, but he was considering it. The kennel workers encouraged him to take the dogs out, or to bring one home for a week as a foster pet. He saw what might have been a husky crossed with a golden retriever—his fur dark brown on the top of his head and his back where a husky's would be black, and an orangish-yellow on the rest of his body where a husky's would be white. The sign on the kennel said his name was Arthur. Wesley guessed his age at three or four years old. Arthur was calm and remarkably dignified considering his circumstances. He didn't bark or spin circles or jump on the gate. He sat and looked up with his bright hazel eyes.

Wesley asked a worker for a leash and a chorus of barking followed them out as he took Arthur to the pathway along the creek behind the shelter. The dog only pulled when he wanted to investigate a scent. He led Wesley down the path under the cottonwoods, walking at an easy pace, curious and alert. The dual pleasure of exercising on a natural path and taking care of a sweet, innocent animal. His problem, though, was his workload wouldn't allow him enough time to give the dog the life he deserved. He didn't have a yard and he wasn't home nearly enough. But would taking him in and keeping him in an apartment be better than the other fate that awaited him if he wasn't adopted?

Wesley decided he'd make his trips to the shelter a regular part of his social media posts and take pictures and leave descriptions of the dogs on his feeds so his friends might be motivated to rescue them. The best compromise he could come up with. At least this was positive.

When he got back to the office he pulled up Instagram, loaded a picture, and wrote the following about Arthur:

There's a beautiful dog down at the shelter. A #verygoodboy. Mature temperament. Doesn't pull much on the leash except to sniff. Healthy coat. Very good with other people. Didn't show any aggression toward other dogs on the pathway, only friendly tail wagging. I can only imagine something happened to his owner because no one would ever give up a dog like this on purpose. He's too big for my apartment. But someone who can walk him and has a decent yard please give him a good home. #dogstagram #huskylife #wesleywalks

The comments were a variation of the dog emoji and hearts, the smiling cat with heart eyes emoji and OMG SO CUTE!!! One of his friends said he'd go to the shelter and check him out and that was about all Wesley could hope for.

17

Danielle was sipping a Manhattan and searching Instagram for new Korean fried chicken restaurants when Flannery walked in. Danielle put her phone down and glanced up with increased frequency until Flannery noticed her and came over. She had shaved off the mohawk and her hair was boyish and dark.

"Are you by yourself?" Flannery asked.

"Sadly, yes." Danielle looked at the bartender and tapped her glass. "This is my spot. I live down the street."

"With your girlfriend."

"It's complicated."

"Is it 'complicated?'" Flannery kept her smile going, a challenge.

"We've known each other a long time." Danielle stirred her ice with her straw.

The guy next to Danielle got up and Flannery took his barstool. When the bartender came back she paid for their round with cash.

"Aren't you here with someone?"

"I was supposed to be, but she's actually meeting someone." Flannery took a drink of her cocktail. "Can I ask you the most important question?"

"Yep."

"Would you ever leave her?"

"I haven't really thought about—"

Flannery leaned over and kissed her. Danielle could taste the alcohol and cigarettes.

"How many of those vodkas have you had?"

"You just looked so cute. C'mon. Let's get a table."

"I'd love to, but I have a full day of paperwork tomorrow. Never start your own company. No days off."

Flannery leaned back and squinted. She stuck out her chin and with the tip of her tongue between her teeth she stood and said, "I guess I'll see you around."

Danielle waited until Flannery walked out then set a $20 bill on the bar and left. She rubbed off any stray lipstick with the back of her hand, thinking about her question, about how no, she wouldn't leave Taylor. They were locked into this life they'd built together.

18.

Taylor and Danielle asked if they could be sat in Henry's section. The hostess took them over to a two-top next to the bar area. The place had more than 50 tables and with wood paneling on the walls was meant to look and feel Old World European.

The menus were laminated with a dozen pages of German-style food. Pretzels, sausages, spätzle, and beer cheese soup. Two full pages with detailed descriptions of the beers on tap. A page in the back dedicated to the story of the brothers who founded the brewery decades ago, before craft beer had become a trend.

"What are you two doing here?" Henry said, smiling. He was wearing a tight-fitting brown T-shirt with the brewery's name on the front. A black apron around his waist was stuffed with check presenter books, pens, and paper-wrapped straws.

"We missed you," Danielle said.

To Taylor, Henry wasn't his normal self. Obviously in work mode. "Let me get you some samples," he said.

He stepped away and stopped to check on an older couple next to them.

"He's probably a pretty good waiter," Taylor said.

"Too smart to be working here."

"He'll figure it out. I've been there. So have you."

"Never again."

Henry came back with a tray and stiffly set down their snifters of beer.

"So this is the hefeweizen. Once you taste the banana in it it'll always taste like bananas to you. I also brought the rye IPA and the chocolate stout."

"Do you like this job?" Danielle asked as she sipped on the yellow beer.

"We get free beer. Do you guys know what you want to eat, or should I help you?"

"Help us," Taylor said. "That would be great."

"You should try the spätzle. Spätzle? I still don't really know how to pronounce that. If you want some meat, the schnitzel. Also the sauerbraten's good."

"Are you just saying random German words now?" Taylor asked.

"Danke. Danke. Gesundheit. I'll give you guys a few minutes.

He went off down the aisle. They sipped their beers from the small glasses.

"I remember eating dinner with my parents one time and we had this old waitress, probably in her 60s," Taylor said. "The place was busy. She was struggling. My mom said, 'Must be really hard at her age.' And my dad said, 'She should've saved her money when she was younger.' Thought that was harsh. I mean, Henry's fine. He'll land a good job. He has experience. He's talented. He wants to work."

When Henry came back they had each finished their samples.

"Any winners?"

"I like stout," Danielle said.

"Yech," Taylor said. "I'll do the hef. I like bananas."

"Food?" Henry asked.

"Everything you mentioned," Danielle said. "All the most German-sounding things. Anything that starts with SH or SCH."

"What time do you get off?" Taylor asked.

"Couple hours. Let's meet up if you're doing something."

He went off to put their order in.

"But seriously, restaurant work sucks. Most of my family worked in restaurants at some point," Danielle said. "Bussed tables. Washed dishes. Couldn't get jobs as waiters unless we knew someone. Even at the Mexican restaurants."

"Better than working in the beet fields."

"Hundred percent. I did it a few times in high school with my cousins. Hardest work ever. Thinning beets." She took a sip of her beer.

"You've never told me about any of this."

"I never talk about it ... do you want to hear about it? So, you had to work out a rhythm, cut out every other beet with a hoe. And the weeds were the worst. Canadian thistle. You'd have to hack your ass off to get them out. Blisters all over my hands. With gloves. I wasn't very good. The old heads were always laughing at me. I wasted a lot of energy. And it was so fucking hot. The smart ones wore loose, lightweight clothing and straw hats. I'd be out there in my swimsuit and jean shorts trying to get a tan."

"Now they just spray Roundup on everything."

"And everyone gets cancer."

A woman with glasses dropped off the hot, soft pretzels and beer cheese and stone ground mustard in a motion so graceful she barely broke stride.

"You should teach Henry how to do that," Taylor said. "He looked like a real farmer setting that tray down last time."

"We like that farmer. He's a good worker."

They pulled apart the pretzel and dipped it in the cheese and mustard.

"I had a job like this in college," Taylor said. "Total shit show. Most of the staff was fucked up at work. Coke in the bathrooms. And after work was even worse. Everybody hooking up. People getting STDs. A lot of drama."

"Sounds like a blast."

"Not pretty."

"Probably what our staff's doing."

"Oh they're definitely boning each other."

Henry brought over the entrées and said, "I'm getting cut in about 30 minutes. Let's go get drinks."

Taylor and Danielle ate and talked about work, about what they needed to get done, personnel problems, plans for the coming weeks, and Henry kept them well-supplied with beer.

When dinner was over, Henry brought their check, heavily discounted. When he went down to the staff room to change, he poured a lager from the staff keg and drank it in three drinks as he swapped out his work clothes for a basic gray T-shirt and jeans.

They were waiting for him at their table when he came back up.

"Let's go around the corner," he said.

Outside it was dark and the sky was still glowing, clear, a cool summer temperature. They went into the dive bar and sat at a horseshoe-shaped booth underneath a neon Coors sign and ordered a pitcher of margaritas.

"Did Danielle tell you what's going on with her?" Taylor said.

"Do I want to know?"

"Nothing is going on with me," Danielle said.

"Not true. Tell Henry about your new friend."

"Nothing to tell."

"She's being shy because she's in love."

Henry leaned back in his chair. He tried to laugh, but Taylor wasn't really being funny.

"Well?" Taylor said, looking at Danielle. "Tell him."

"You don't have to," Henry said.

"Fine. I was starting to become sorta friends with a girl from the club."

"Which one?"

"See. Now Henry's interested."

"Malice. But that's not her real name."

"It's Flannery," Taylor said. "Which—what kind of name is that, anyway?"

"The one with the big hair? The mohawk?"

"She shaved it off. Look, I didn't 'fall in love with a stripper.'"

"You're blushing!" Taylor said.

"Why are you making this such a big deal?"

"I'm not. But you're acting like nothing's happening, and it obviously is."

Henry shifted himself in his chair and took a drink. "Sounds like you two need to talk this out."

"Oh, not at all," Danielle said.

"She's trying to change the subject," Taylor said.

"I'm pretty tired," Henry said. "I told myself I was just going to have a couple of drinks."

"You're making Henry feel awkward," Danielle said. "It's Saturday night and he's talking about going home."

"Henry? Henry's a guy. I'm sure he'd love the details about all of this. I'm the one who feels awkward."

"That's obvious."

"That's obvious? You're trying to fuck a stripper and you still want to sleep in our bed."

"Jesus, Taylor," Henry said. "I thought you two had an arrangement?"

"We do," Taylor said. "But no one said anything about strippers. That wasn't in the fine print."

"This isn't fun. You're being mean."

"I'll get the check," Henry said. "Since you came all the way to see me."

He paid, and as he was walking out he looked back and they were sitting there staring at each other. Taylor was leaned back in the booth with her chin tilted upward and Danielle's expression read *what the fuck*.

19.

Henry biked to work the next morning. The air had a sharp, metallic smell. When he arrived he went through his routine: Opened the gates, rolled up the door to the dock, turned on the computer, got the forklift from the warehouse. The work order on the clipboard meant he had ten kegs to take from the brewery over to the restaurant. He drove the forklift down the ramp into the cooler and checked the clipboard until he found the keg of hazy IPA. It was sitting alone on a pallet. He forked that pallet and brought it down. He threw other kegs—amber ale, milk stout, lager—down from the stack onto the tire absorbing each barrel's fall. He rolled them over and stacked them on the pallet. After building the stack of eight, four on each pallet, he drove it over to the restaurant's back entrance. Needing two more to complete the order, he walked back to the dock, grabbed the hand truck, and wheeled it down into the cooler. He rolled a por-ter keg a few feet to the hand truck and stood it up, tilted it and slid the tongue of the cart under it. The metal slipped under quick and sharp. *Ssinnnt*. He hooked the keg in place. The second and final keg was on the third row of the sour beers. He climbed up the barrels and pulled it down, landing it on the rubber tire. It thudded with a dead, heavy sound. He rolled the hand truck over. He bent down to pick it up. As he strained to lift it onto the upright keg, as he had done dozens of times, a sharp pain erupted in the muscle running from his right shoulder blade down to his right hip, along the spine. The muscle contracted and adjusted his posture.

At first he thought it was only a tweak. After the initial shock and pain, he went on with his work. He wheeled the kegs over to the restaurant elevator and loaded them into the cooler. He drove the forklift onto the dock and took the clipboard down to the cooler to mark the inventory and take the empty pallets out to the yard. As he pulled a pallet down, his back muscle twitched and he fell to his knees. He winced as he took off his jacket and felt his back. The muscle had swelled, and it bulged from his shoulder blade to his hip. The blood left his face. Saliva pooled around his tongue. Then the real pain came. He shuffled to the restaurant and told Jeannette what had happened.

"Not the first time," she said. She called Gary and had him come in to finish the shift. She told Henry to go home and make an appointment with a doctor.

Two days later, after bed rest and ibuprofen that wasn't much help, he rode a bus east to a physical therapy clinic. The therapist gave him a massage and had him do lat pulldowns, upright rows, and straight-arm pulldowns on the cable machine with a moderate amount of weight to stretch and strengthen the muscles. He showed Henry two stretches, one called Child's Pose, where he would kneel and sit back on his feet then stretch his arms out with his palms touching the floor.

"You're going to have some persistent problems," the therapist said. "Your ribs have been displaced on your right side. Do the stretches. Do the exercises. You'll get some relief, but it'll take time."

They gave him a prescription for a heavy muscle relaxer and oxycontin painkillers his coworkers would buy if he stopped needing them. The doctor said he could wait tables if he didn't carry anything too heavy. That night he opened the dock and manned the keg delivery station—he just had to radio a warehouse guy that he needed help hauling kegs to either the restaurant or to a customer's car.

One brewery worker, a hulking man with SCOTT sewed onto a patch on his blue overalls, caught up with Henry by the wort chiller and told him he also had that job until he hurt his back. "Still not right," Scott said. "It's a burn job. The only guy that does it full time is Gary. He's holding out to get in the warehouse. He won't be too happy when you tell him you're on injured reserve. His back's screwed up, too."

When Henry finished his shift he went down to the lockers and poured a beer from the staff keg. John came by and said, "Couldn't hack it on the dock, bro?"

"Cheers," Henry said.

"Actually, you're like the fifth guy to have that job since I've worked here. They all get hurt. So keep your head up. You're not Superman."

After his beer, Henry went back over to the dock. Gary was in the cooler with a clipboard doing his end-of-the-day inventory.

"Hey, man," Henry said. "Some bad news."

"Yuh. I heard," Gary said, moving with his robotic hustle over to the stacked pallets.

"Sorry if it means you're stuck with extra work. Must have lifted wrong."

"Yuh. Happens," he said, walking up to the gate and pulling down the chain to roll the metal down.

"Mike knows what's going on with the schedule and—"

Gary shook his head and waved him off. "Yuuuh. I'm really busy. Have to get this done. Not all of us are on worker's comp."

He walked past Henry and hopped on the forklift to park it and charge the battery. Henry called an Uber that cost him two hours of work just to get home. Throwing out his back when he was making his living doing manual labor was demoralizing. It robbed him of the comfort that his strength and health could always land him work. Take that away from him in a place where there were too few sit-down jobs for a generation of college-educated workers and he started looking for a way out. He had left America once with the naive thought it would be there when he came back. That it would be unchanged, the cities the same way and the people doing the same things. He thought he could have his old life again. The problem was living elsewhere changed him. He no longer cared as much about trying to compete in this society. There were other ways to live. Other cultures in the world where he could go to reinvent himself as anything he wanted. Expat life had its charms. There certainly was a lot less shame in being poor and having a mediocre job in a foreign country that was indifferent at best, hostile at worst, to his success and status. He'd learned all of that, learned where the exit door was. All he needed to do was to step through it, to get on a plane for Asia, or anywhere, really, and he'd be free of these societal constraints. That knowledge gave him comfort. It also made him far less likely to stay where he was and make the best of it.

20.

––––––––––––––––

"Hey, girl. Can you tell me if Flannery is working?" Danielle asked, lining up ten one dollar bills end to end in front of her.

The corner of Cricket's mouth twisted as she slipped the bills into her waist band. "Back in like an hour," she said, and rolled away.

Danielle leaned down and hit her vape pen. The THC tightened up her eyes. Cricket ended her song, scooping up the bills off the floor, gathering her clothing and holding it all in her arms against her chest like a bundle of firewood.

Danielle went to the bar and talked to the bartender with collagen lips and breast implants, straight black hair, Betty Page-core. They chatted until Flannery came to the bar and gave her a hug, wearing a green wig and green eyeshadow.

"What are you doing here?" Flannery asked.

"You don't check your texts?" Danielle said.

"Look at you. Are you trying to get possessive? How cute. Let's step out here."

They walked outside and stood under the awning. The wind had started to blow. Flannery cupped her hands and turned to the wall to light a cigarette. Danielle liked how fake she looked in her wig and makeup.

"When are you off?"

"I'm done. Not into it tonight. I danced once before you got here and they kept screwing up the music. No money in the crowd. Not worth it."

"Oh cool. Home then?"

"I think so. Want to come back to my place? I have weed. Not that you don't."

"Sure. Sounds fun."

"I'm going back in to get my stuff. You can't leave with me. My boss will get pissed. But I'll text my address."

They went back inside and Danielle stood at the corner of the bar, watching the bartender work, feeling like a balloon with a slow leak. After a couple of minutes, Flannery came up from behind and touched her on the elbow.

"Check your phone. I'll see you soon," she said.

Danielle walked up to the bar for a shot of tequila. Betty Page set it on the bar and said, "I don't think I need to tell you this, but if you hurt her I'll kill you."

The Uber driver asked questions, and Danielle answered them in noncommittal, short, distracted mutters. He had a disco ball hanging from his rearview mirror, the only detail Danielle noticed. The amount of energy she had in anticipation. Imagine your crush had been dancing for you naked for hours and hours and you had not touched them. Imagine you had been tied up, and now you were untied.

At the house, she knocked at the front door. No answer. She went around to the side door and a small dog growled. The stereo played Devendra Banhart loud. From the window, the house smelled of nag champa and pot. She texted and Flannery responded that she was showering and to come in.

Danielle opened the door and went down the hall to the cluttered kitchen. Flannery lived with roommates, the house decorated in a kaleidoscope of psychedelic tapestries and strange lamps. She found a bottle of red wine and twisted off the cap and drank. There was a half-smoked joint still smoldering in an ashtray. She put it down when Flannery came in wearing a robe, her hair wet from the shower and smelling like cherry blossoms.

Flannery hopped onto the counter and when Danielle kissed her she wrapped her legs around her waist.

"You taste like weed," Flannery said.

"Found some on the counter. And some wine."

They went into the bedroom, and Flannery drank from the bottle of wine and kissed her with a mouthful.

Danielle unwrapped her robe and knelt. She stayed down for a while, then looked up and asked, "Is that OK?"

Flannery said yes and Danielle drank from the bottle.

Danielle stopped, pulled her head up and leaned back, inviting Flannery to trade positions. Flannery slowly got on her knees and all of her tattoos and everything else. But Flannery wasn't trying.

"What's wrong?" Danielle asked.

"No, you're beautiful. Perfect," Flannery said. "But I'm tired. I think I'd rather just get high."

"Is this a 'chefs don't cook at home' situation?"

"I'm not a prostitute."

"You know what I mean."

"I'm exhausted. Let's finish that joint."

They went into the living room and sat on opposite ends of the couch. Danielle wanted nothing at all to do with the pot. She could get an endless amount of that. This gorgeous, interesting, independent woman was sitting right there. But she had tried, so she had no other choice but to smoke and sink into the couch, their legs intertwined, the freak folk on the stereo not soothing enough. Danielle wanted so much more than this.

She stayed until the joint was finished, drank a glass of water, then called a car. Inside the cab she looked out the window, wondering what she had done wrong. She opened her messaging app and waited for Flannery to text her. She drafted a message that said, "That was nice, but what happened?" But what if Flannery didn't respond to that? Then what? Then it really was over. And she wasn't ready for that.

She sat back and breathed in the Nissan Altima's fake

strawberry air freshener and scrolled through her feeds. It was past midnight, but what did time have to do with anything? She would go home and scroll and scroll and scroll until she wasn't thinking about her life anymore, until she couldn't feel this reality, then she would sleep.

21

Henry turned on the lamp and sat up, feeling weird, not hungover or more dehydrated than usual, no immediate need to use the bathroom. His back hurt, but not any worse than before. It was the skin on his left arm. He pulled it from the covers and held it under the light, where he could see a line of sores running from the back of his thumb to halfway up his forearm. He tried to convince himself they were spider bites, or that the mollescum had spread to his arm, but he knew. These spots were different. He'd been in enough cheap hostels and woken up with similar welts.

He stripped all the blankets and sheets off the bed. A black bug the shape of an apple seed scurried to the corner of the mattress. He pinched it, and his own blood coated his fingertips. He went out to the couch and tried to sleep, but when he closed his eyes he dreamed of a swarm of bedbugs pouring down from the ceiling and devouring him.

In the morning, he went to the property manager's office on the first floor and knocked. The overweight man with gray hair and a beard glared at him over his crossword puzzle.

"The building has bed bugs," Henry said.

"Not the first time. We can have someone come spray 'em. 'Bout all we can do aside from burning this place to the ground."

"I'm going to need out of my lease."

"You'll have to pay the fee to break it."

"That doesn't work for me."

"Nothing I can do."

"How about this? Let me break my lease or I'm going to register this property in every bedbug registry on the internet, post about it on Reddit and social media, and call the local news outlets."

"Fine. Fine. We can get you out."

Henry went back up to this room. He brushed his teeth as he ran the shower and let it get hot. He looked at himself in the mirror and thought *you're young, in good health, in spite of the hint of dark patches in the corners of your eyes and your back. At least your beard shores up the slow erosion of your jawline. You can make a few more fresh starts.*

But what was his next move? Did he even want to stay here? Wasn't that the eternal question? Where to live? This city had a good music scene. Fun neighborhoods. Beautiful murals in the alleys behind the breweries. A monthly art walk. People from all over the country—a lot from the Midwest and the South—moved here. But it was still painfully white and leaned more and more conservative as you left the city. Large swaths of red-blooded, rural America. Shared ideals with the states to the east. Pickup trucks and guns and nationalism. The mountains gave the state another identity, another culture. One of camping, hiking, skiing and snowboarding. Shared ideals with cities in the public-land states to the west. SUVs and rooftop tents and environmentalism. Swirling in the middle was the city's urban character. Food trucks in the parking lots sold upscale hamburgers, arepas, pupusas, gruyere mac and cheese. The city's relationship with jazz went all the way back to the early days, when brass horns blew in basement clubs in the small hours of the night. Music from some of the best bands in the country echoed in the canyons surrounding Red Rocks. The main museum curated modern exhibitions with the art world's most exciting young stars. The city had become a relevant contributor to the country's culture. Motorized scooters and loft apartments and political activism. He'd arrived in one of the most interesting cities in America right as it was undergoing a major transformation. Plus, weed was legal.

He responded to an ad on Facebook for a room close to Colfax in Capitol Hill. A woman named Betty managed the property and she interviewed him that morning, sitting across from him on the worn, living room couch. She was probably in her 50s, of Southeast Asian descent, and wore gray sweatpants with UCLA BRUINS on the legs and a red sweatshirt with the stencil outline of a monkey's face.

"What do you do?" she asked.

"I'm freelancing. Writing. Working at a restaurant."

"You'd fit right in. We have musicians, poets, artists. Younger than you, just out of college. But you'll get along fine. You can do whatever you want, but if you start having guests stay over they have to pay rent, too."

Betty took him up to a bedroom with a twin bed, writing desk, closet, and old-fashioned baseboard heater. They toured the kitchen and living area with vintage furniture and one piece of abstract art on the wall—red lines on a gray-brown background. He said he'd take the room. She only wanted $600 a month. He'd been paying $1,200 for his infested apartment.

"You have a floormate, Charles. Everyone calls him Chuck D. Nicest guy. Works in a restaurant in Uptown. A fancy cocktail bar with expensive steaks. He wants to be a chef. Always up here trying new recipes. Lucky for you." She paused. "You'll be perfect. Move in. Write something beautiful."

Henry left his bike there, walked back to his apartment, packed up his stuff, and took an Uber back to the house with his backpack and laptop bag. Aside from his clothes, all he still had were a few books and a laptop. As he was hanging up his shirts there was a knock on the door. A tall man about the same age, late 20s, stood in the doorway. He wore a blonde goatee and his brown eyes blinked under wire-frame glasses.

"Everything you ever wanted, right?" he said.

They shook hands in a clumsy, stilted manner, their hands not really lining up right.

Henry hung up a brown jacket he had custom-made for $15 in Hoi An. "I've heard good things about the restaurant you work at."

"It's a good spot. What are you doing for work?"

"I'm working at a brewery. Writing for a few places online."

"How's that going?"

"Not great. Any jobs at your restaurant? I could use a different gig."

"We could always use some help."

Henry closed the door and sat alone in the room. The only window looked into the alley and the back of a three-story, brick apartment building. A guy down there dug through a dumpster, singing to himself in falsetto. The man switched to an impression of Mickey Mouse's voice, a schizophrenic dialogue between two cartoon mice, then to hardcore gangster rap, with lyrics like, "Gonna get this muthafuckin' trash, gonna get this paper, gonna find the good shit for all the trash hoes in all my trash rows." Into a spot-on Elvis impression, saying "the funny thing is, uh hunh, uh hunh, I ain't broke. I ain't nothin' but a hound dog. I found $300 in the dumpster. 20 minutes of work. Half your weekly pay. And I hope you heard me say that. Uh hunh uh hunh. Cuz you're fucking trr raaassshhh." Back to Mickey Mouse.

Henry leaned back on his bed and decided he couldn't watch the ceiling fan as the dumpster performance rattled on. He went out onto the sidewalk, cars parallel parked as close as possible to each other down the street, electric scooters and e-bikes strewn here and there, owners walking dogs with headphones in. From the street, the corner bar smelled like the Wednesday special all-you-can-eat chicken wings. Dudes in flatbill hats congealed inside. He continued on to the vegan restaurant with the dark back bar and a painting of William Burroughs on the wall.

He tried his best to appreciate the beauty of the negroni sitting in front of him. He hadn't tasted the simple bitter red cocktail in years, and the fragrance of the curled orange rind took him all the way back to the night market in Phnom Penh, where he had bought a plate of fresh fruit, some of it unknown to him, and sat cross legged on a patch of concrete with five other foreigners from four different countries, drinking beer and eating oranges, talking about what city, what country they were visiting next. Life was so much simpler, so much easier. If he had all the money he could spend that's how he'd spend it. Traveling the world from country to country. But here he was, broke in the USA. Injured without health insurance or any real job prospects.

Simply sitting in a bar was an exercise in concentration. Overseas he had been accustomed to the language spoken around him forming incomprehensible background noise. The wall of indecipherable sound made it easier to think, not more difficult. He could read or write anywhere without becoming distracted by unintentional eavesdropping when no one spoke English. An effort to block out the conversations around him hadn't been necessary for a while—it was necessary now. He accepted the world could not be filtered and let it pass through him.

And yet the bartenders could make any drink he wanted. People smoked legal joints and vape pens on the street. The jukebox played music he loved, songs he hadn't heard outside of his headphones the entire time he was away.

There were so many small pleasures to appreciate as he waited for the readjustments to occur. He sat back in his chair, took another sip, and re-experienced his old life all while feeling himself embarking on this new one.

On Thursday evening, Henry boiled water in a ceramic pot on the stove. The sun had set and he wasn't scheduled to work. He had some loose leaf oolong tea from a market in Hong Kong and he poured the boiling water into a cup directly over the leaves and let it steep. As he waited for the tea to cool, the shadows changed fast, growing across the wall. Soft laughter from the living room below.

When he came down a woman slightly younger than him sat on the couch giggling and lightly puffing on a device the size of a USB thumb drive. A blue flower-pattern lit up on the top when she inhaled from it. She let out a cloud of vapor. He held up his tea mug.

"Hey, new guy. Betty told me all about you," she said. She wore circular, tortoise-shell glasses and her red hair was parted in the middle. She took another hit and turned her head while she filmed herself exhaling. She tapped her screen a few times then squeezed it to lock. She stood up and said, "Erica," and they shook hands. "Where were you before?"

"Asia. Korea."

"Nice. I've always wanted to live abroad. How's the weed over there?"

"Not good. Hard to find."

"Gross. Maybe not then." She handed Henry the vape pen with a look on her face like she was doing him a favor, giving a coughing man a drink. It tasted like synthetic pineapple and some other petroleum flavor.

"Do you have big plans tonight with your, what is that, tea?"

"Not at all."

"I have an extra ticket to a show. My friend got sick and bailed. We were just texting. You want it?"

"Sure. Why not?"

"Love it. Give me 10 minutes then let's call a car."

He went upstairs and changed into a blue T-shirt and dark gray chinos. When he went back down, Erica was waiting out on the porch.

The Uber ride was nice, sitting in the back of a Jeep Cherokee with the windows down. The August air was warm and the driver said he didn't mind when Erica asked if she could vape. They took a few puffs of her pen as they drove south on the interstate. She asked the driver to play Gregory Alan Isakov, and Henry wanted to let her enjoy the song so he relaxed in his seat and let the scenery-matching music overwhelm his imagination. He was up in the air, floating. He looked over the houses and the old trees and farther east where there were new homes, small trees, the dirt movers and the white tent peaks of the airport then nothing but land and sky all the way to his homeland.

The driver dropped them off at an open-air venue in the middle of an industrial-looking neighborhood, with a wide lawn that sloped down to the reserved seats on wooden risers. It was already crowded, most of the groups had spread out blankets and taken the best spots. They sat at the top of the grass and watched the crowd. Mostly white. A lot of groups of women without men who wore flowers in their hair and headbands, dresses, and earrings with patterns influenced by Native American culture. The men dressed as though they had just come down from the mountains—jeans, caps with the brand names of outdoor gear or sports teams, a lot of plaid and boots. They drank tall cans of craft beer and margaritas or other mixed drinks.

The band emerged to purple stage lights shining through the machine-made fog and crowd-generated pot smoke and vapor. Bands of violet color rose up the screen behind the stage and above it, dots of city lights and beyond those the jagged car key horizon of white dusted mountain tops. The singer yelped and stomped and beat his acoustic guitar. The music felt right for the moment—exactly the type of band and crowd and scene people would have imagined before they had moved here. A few songs in, Erica said, "Some of my other friends just showed up. I'm going to go find them." The opposite of an invitation, and she had already been generous enough. Henry said, "Sure. Thanks for the ticket," and sat back and listened. The sky darkened and the stars came out and he felt reassured.

Henry decided he couldn't keep working at the brewery. His whole identity was built around being strong, a classic man, and after he got hurt everyone saw it was all bullshit. River, who he had flirted with whenever they worked together, was rolling silverware next to him and said, "I thought you were this tough farm kid. Big muscles. Turns out not so strong, huh?"

He scanned Indeed that night until found a gig working at a psychiatric clinic. This would be good material for stories. He applied over the weekend, got a call back Monday morning, and took the bus out to the east side of the city that afternoon to the working-class neighborhoods. Small, old houses. Beat-up cars in the street. Where the people lived who made the hipsters' brunch.

The clinic was a one-story building with several wings sprawling back into a dark grove of pine trees—like a school but less cheerful. To one side was a section of apartments with mailboxes next to the front doors. He went in and announced himself on the intercom and someone somewhere buzzed him in. He was greeted by a short, bald man who led him back to his corner office. Henry was wearing a black suit he had made in Vietnam, which was probably too fancy for the occasion, but was the only clothing he owned that would work for this type of interview.

The man, wearing a smart outfit with a tie and neatly pressed slacks, sat behind his desk and explained the job. Henry would help take care of the clients. They were careful not to call them patients—they didn't want the place to feel like a hospital. This included leading groups and facilitating meals. Conflict resolution was a big part of the job, the man said.

"What else do you do outside of work?" he asked.

"Hobbies? I read and write."

"What do you write?"

"Journalism. Fiction."

"Good. You need some type of release to survive this job."

The man took Henry on a facility tour. He confirmed some clients lived in the apartments. Mostly they were addicts who had washed up in halfway houses and other mentally ill people—a type of clinical purgatory. Some people had come through the system, others had left and come back when they saw what was waiting for them out there.

The man was paged over the intercom and had to take a call in his office.

"Wait here, please," he said.

Henry sat in a metal chair at a folding table in the snack area outside of the cafeteria. The place was calm, clean, and quiet, just like a hospital.

In came a large man, bald save for the hair on the back of his head and over his ears, which he wore long and brown. A filthy white sweatshirt stretched tight over his stomach. He walked in quickly, with a bowed, driven gait, scanning the room before focusing his attention on Henry. He smelled like he hadn't bathed for many days.

"God. God," the man said. "I fucking went down to the corner for milk and almost put my foot through the glass, through the fucking window, with that fucking stupid woman and shit if she was trying to get something from me, trying to get me to say something I fucking wanted to hear. How the fuck am I supposed to know what she wanted to ... fuck, fuck, fuck ... do you have five dollars? I'm good for it. I left my wallet at Tim's and he left and locked up his house before I had a chance to get it. It's just over there. It's just ... I don't know if I like the way you look. The way you're looking at me. You're starting to make me kind of mad. Making me feel stupid. Fuccccccck you."

"I'm sorry," Henry said. He sat up and the muscle in his back spasmed. He gritted his teeth. He should have taken another pain pill.

"I bet you're one of those condescending types. One of those, one of those suits. I don't like your suit. You look like a motherfucking undertaker. An underfucker ... Do you have five fucking dollars?"

He stood over Henry and Henry could smell that sweatshirt, rotten and unclean, the smell of shit and sweat and earth. "Sam! Hey, this is Henry." The interviewer came back. "He's interviewing with us today. Hope you weren't too hard on him."

Sam backed away from the short man and stood against the wall, meek now, looking down.

"You can go," the man said, and Sam shuffled away.

They finished the tour, and when the man asked Henry if he had any questions he said he did not.

When the director called a week later to offer Henry a job he politely declined, said he was moving back overseas. Costa Rica sounded good. Paris loomed in his imagination. He'd probably go back to Korea. National health care and no drug scene. This city had been good, then it had injured him in a way he would deal with for years, if not the rest of his life. But he wasn't ready to leave yet. First, he'd talk to Taylor and Danielle about a job.

22.

Danielle waited on the porch in hiking shoes, holding a blue plastic water bottle and stretching her calf muscles. Flannery drove up in a lifted, silver Ram truck with two dogs in the back seat, a malamute and a Bernese mountain dog smiling through the open window.

Repressed love, or lust, never really dies. If it's not acted on, it becomes compact and hard, a dried jasmine lotus ball, and you can store it away, but you can never be rid of it. You keep it there, hopeful that one day you'll be able to add hot water to it and watch the petals unfurl. Then you can drink.

Danielle got in and went along for the ride.

"How's the business coming?" Flannery asked as she drove out of the city.

"Busy. I probably shouldn't be taking the day off."

"You want me to drop you off at work?"

"No. Fuck no. Just—owning your own business —"

"Not the move."

"Not at all."

Flannery turned the radio up—the indie station was playing Tycho—and they settled into the drive. There was a lot of traffic on the interstate. Danielle sat watching the cars and blaming herself for letting the energy between them die. Flannery was wearing the earrings Danielle had given her, the ones she had bought from a Creole vendor in New Orleans. Suns made of wood and hand-painted yellow. She exited and the road wound upward through forest until it leveled off and the scenery opened up. She parked at the trailhead next to a historic homestead. A house and a barn and two smaller outbuildings had been converted into a wedding venue. Flannery took the Bernese and Danielle the malamute. The trail was mostly flat. The state park was a former ranch and had been donated to the government as public land. They hiked through grasslands toward a hogback and a grove of pines. Forest fire haze muted the sun. There weren't many other people on the trail. A few hikers, a few people on electric bikes.

"So obviously you're back with what's-his-name?"

"Paul? Sort of. I don't know."

Danielle paused at a pine tree next to the trail to breathe in its butterscotch-scented trunk.

"But you still have feelings for him."

"I still love everyone I've ever been with. Don't you?"

"No. No—that would suck."

Flannery bit the mouthpiece of her hydration pack, filled her mouth with water, then spit it out.

"Do you want to come over after this and meet him? I have to take the dogs and truck back to his place."

"Sounds awkward."

"He knows about you."

"Let me think about it."

The trail grew steeper as they approached the ridgeline. Danielle was breathing through her mouth now. Her quads and calves burned as they trudged back and forth on the switchback trails. They hadn't seen anyone for about half an hour so they let the dogs off their leashes and they loped on ahead up the trail, Flannery calling them back if they went out of sight. They crested the ridge and looked back east toward the city on the plain.

"Whoa. When did that happen?" Flannery asked. Below them, where the spine of rocks and trees sloped back downward to the grassland, the flatland was blackened and charred.

"I can't keep track anymore," Danielle said.

They could make out a gray trail through the dark land so they descended and went on. The burnt pasture wasn't hot; the fire wasn't that recent. But when the wind gusted plumes of ash rose into the air. The dogs stuck to the trail, not interested in exploring the soot and char.

They went on through the blackened pasture, following the trail as it looped back around toward the trailhead.

"Come back to our place," Flannery said. "We'll have drinks and dinner."

Danielle said, "Sure. All right."

They finished the hike and drove back to the city. Flannery parked the truck in a pay lot and they walked with the dogs to the townhouse. A man had clearly decorated the place. Stained-wood wall art made from an old pallet hung over a large TV. A folded American flag in a triangle case sat on the mantle above the fireplace. Elk antlers hung above the door to the hallway. Other than that not much on the walls.

They began dinner with a bottle of wine as the meat finished on the smoker, sharing travel stories, talking about the world. Paul mentioned one assignment hunting an operative in Saudi Arabia. He talked about combat and about the health problems caused by burn pits. When he learned what Danielle did for a living he mentioned some of his military buddies were using medical marijuana for PTSD.

"I have a buddy who does that, too," she said.

"It is Denver. Probably a lot of them," he said. "I can't do weed, though. Me and paranoia don't mix."

"I couldn't do the military," Danielle said.

"Of course you could," Paul said. "Look at you. You'd do great."

They ate the slices of brisket he had smoked and drank more cheap bottles of red wine, trying to work out the dynamic between them. Paul had the composed energy of someone who had lived under intense conditions. Danielle had lost, but she wasn't willing to admit that to herself yet. Flannery bringing her there was her way of showing Danielle why she should give up.

23

Taylor didn't have much to load in—guitar, a music stand, and an amp. Henry and Danielle helped her carry the gear from her car to a room behind the stage in the warehouse. They weren't familiar with the bands playing before her so they went to a club across the street for a beer. It was about 5:30 and hot, the weeds in the sidewalk cracks green and healthy. The air was dry, the sky hazy.

Their college buddy Brian was in town from Omaha. He met them at the club with a dark-haired girl who was pretty and much younger. They sat in a curved upholstered leather booth. Brian wore a trucker hat with BRANSON on it that pushed down his curly brown hair until it bunched up around his ears. His beard was tangled and greasy and he wore a blue hooded sweatshirt with the sleeves cut off and a mustard stain on the chest. He was sort of famous and that explained the girl.

"How much do you think it would cost to get one of the girls to come over here and just talk to me?" Brian said. "'Honey, I don't want a dance. Just a talk. A lap talk.' How much do you think a lap talk costs?"

They laughed and sipped their drinks. Taylor was thinking about her upcoming set. She remembered Brian from open mic nights in college, when he was singing old outlaw country tunes—Waylon Jennings, Merle Haggard, that era. Brian, in Taylor's words, had "gone further" since. His face showed years of traveling in America. A lot of Greyhound trips. It had given him a road quality, a kind of grounded, comfortable manliness that suited him. He had picked up this way of saying "shit yes" from somewhere. He said it as an affirmative, as a question, or a simple space filler.

"Should we get a pitcher of beer?" "Shit yes."

"I think I'm going home for a while?" "Shit yes?"

"You hear that new Phosphorescent record?" "Shit. Yes. So good."

Taylor saw Brian three times that year and each time he was wearing the same hat and cut-off sweatshirt. Only the length of his beard varied. Always a different girl with him. Some free, sweet girl there for the music. He had so much promise as a songwriter back then when he was working a lot, writing songs on his phone. Taylor watched how Henry stared at Brian as he spoke and laughed at all of his sayings, even when he wasn't trying to be funny.

Taylor had one drink then left and went back to the venue. She tuned her guitar and went over the setlist. She could hear the all-woman rock group ending their set through the walls. She practiced for about 15 more minutes before she came out. She had a quiet room full of kids waiting for her. She knelt and sat down on her heels and sang with her guitar in her lap. Her songs were life songs, about pain and strength and the people in her world. She sang about summer and Western skies and getting on the road just to leave. That old cure she had tried several times already, but it hadn't stuck. There were probably about 30 people in the crowd, and everyone was listening closely.

After the third song, she broke the top string on her guitar. She was too nervous to try to restring it and tune in front of the crowd, so she folded it back and kept playing, the chords missing that high note. When she was playing she thought only about the music, not work or the trouble they might be in—nothing but making sure she played the songs right. And the sense of relief when it was over.

She gave what she could and when it was over they clapped. She felt like she had been holding her breath the whole time. She bowed and said thank you then another band came on.

After all the bands had played Henry helped Taylor load up her stuff. He was carrying out the amp as she stuffed the guitar into her car.

"You did great," he said. "Played through that busted string like a total pro."

"That was awful," she said.

Danielle wound up a cord and threw it in the back. "We're going back to our house if you want to come?"

"I'm good," Henry said. "On the job hunt tomorrow. Need to find something soon."

"Our offer still stands," Danielle said.

"I appreciate that. We'll see."

Danielle drove them back to their house. The city felt raw and loud to Taylor—alive and hopeful. It was warm, people were out, and despite how tired she was she considered closing down a bar. But that would mean finding parking and a place to sit and waiting for drinks. The feeling passed and she rolled down her window, let the night air wash over her.

Back at their house, Taylor opened a bottle of sauvignon blanc and took it out on the porch. When Danielle joined her Taylor asked, "Do you think we'll still be friends when we're older?" On the street, cars went by with ride-share lights in the windshields. "Because people change. Have other lives. Careers. Fall in love. Move around. I don't know ..." Danielle was frowning. "Sorry. I'm just in a mood. I mean, I see my parents, who still have their friends around them at their age, and I want that. That's good for them. But it's different when you stay in one place your whole life. We're all spread out. We're friends on Instagram or whatever, but I don't really ever talk to anyone on there. Do you ever just call your old friends? I don't. I wouldn't know what to say."

Taylor picked up her wine glass, refilled it, and took a sip.

She sat on the bench and Danielle leaned against the railing.

"I don't call my own mom enough," Danielle said. "That's terrible. I need to go see her."

Two dudes with backwards, flat-billed caps sped by on electric scooters, talking loudly, excited.

"The only real chance we have at staying friends is to live close to each other," Taylor said. "Email and phone calls and texts aren't enough. It's too easy to just let that go. I mean, people can visit. But that's not the same."

Danielle looked at her feet and tilted her head. Taylor glanced at her, waiting for her to work herself up to what she wanted to say.

"Flannery ghosted me," Danielle said. "How pathetic does that sound?"

Taylor leaned over and topped off Danielle's glass.

"Just stopped responding. I sent a couple of texts and called once and nothing. Gone."

Taylor rubbed her hand down her throat. "Did you have real feelings for her?"

"Probably not," Danielle turned away from Taylor and faced the street.

"Look, don't take this the wrong way. But. Considering how you met, this is what you thought would happen, right?"

"Yeah. Of course. I'm not stupid." Danielle stood up and stretched her arms over her head. "But I mean, what the fuck. She can't just ignore me."

Taylor leaned back on the bench and tilted her head to the side, stretched her neck. She sat down on her feet on the rug. Leaned forward and extended both palms out as far as she could on the ground, slowly stretching from side to side.

Danielle finished her glass of wine. "I thought this whole thing would be good stress relief. It's been the exact opposite."

"What if you took up kickboxing again?"

"What we need to do is make sure we're not going to jail, so we're not stressed out all the time. Make it go away."

"I wish I could make it go away."

Danielle shook the empty bottle. "We should sit down and define our exit strategy. Set a timeline. Something like—in five years we're out. No matter what."

"I'll be amazed if we can make it that long."

Danielle stood and went to the kitchen where she filled the kettle from the Britta pitcher. Taylor leaned back, on her hands. The noise from the kettle grew slowly. Danielle came out and said, "I'm making chamomile."

Taylor went up to her room and got ready for bed. She read from a Sally Rooney novel, but she was too tired and she could only get through a couple of pages. Before she went to sleep she checked her social feeds. She set her phone to Do Not Disturb, set the alarm for six, hit play on the white noise app, and turned off the light before Danielle came up.

24.

The office manager brought Wesley a stack of invoices, receipts, and other business-related letters. He finished going over the inventory spreadsheet then went through the envelopes one at a time. He examined the energy bill, aware one of their biggest expenses was power consumption, and noted the new HVAC system was indeed working as efficiently as promised by the company that had sold it to them. The bill for the synthetic nutrient mixture was too high so he made a note on his running To-Do list next to his computer—Look into cost of mixing our own fertilizer.

He rifled through more spam mail and advertisements until another letter from the Marijuana Enforcement Division stamped with FINAL NOTICE caught his attention. The letter was written in the same clear language for a government document as the one from two weeks ago. Another simple warning explaining it had come to the attention of state cannabis regulators that Sugar Magnolia was promoting the purchase of more than the legal daily allotment of marijuana—one ounce per adult-use customer, per transaction—and the company should immediately cease and desist from any such activities. He reread it, then he ran it through the paper shredder.

When the work was handled he drove to the animal shelter. The wind had picked up and blown the wildfire smoke away from the city, so the day was hot and clear. The workers were friendly to him when he arrived. Someone had rescued the Husky-mix, Arthur, so Wesley picked Momo, a gray, white, and black speckled Australian shepherd with one blue eye and one brown, and hooked up a leash. Momo jumped, spun a circle, and barked out of uncontained excitement. His lack of a tail didn't keep him from wiggling his backend like a happy, docked lamb.

Together, they took to the sidewalk down the hill past the Victorian, turreted mansions. The green tree branches curved overhead and formed a canopy. Momo sniffed at a bike rack and pissed on the frame of a Cannondale stripped of its seat and wheels. The dog was less than 40 pounds, but a squirrel or rabbit crossing his path gave him strength for his size, and twice he pulled Wesley toward the street after a fleeing cat.

Once Momo's first burst of energy subsided, Wesley more easily controlled him. They walked at a steady clip down the hill toward the governor's mansion. Passed the gated grounds of the palatial estate and into a city park—it was after five and a dozen or so dogs and their owners milled around. The dogs formed groups of two or three and ran and wrestled. Some played fetch with their owners. Others sat staring up at the squirrels in the treetops. A few found sticks to chew. Many of the dogs spent their days in apartments while their owners worked. This was as close to being free as they could get in a day.

Wesley unleashed Momo and he took off at full speed, his paws only lightly touching the grass, to confront a white malamute-mix with blue eyes. The malamute crouched with its front legs splayed in a clear challenge, welcoming Momo to attack or engage in any way he saw fit. Momo crashed into the other dog, spun, barked, and the white dog ran away, Momo chasing in a wide arc up onto the lawn of the mansion on the hill and back behind Wesley and around again.

"His favorite game," said a tallish guy wearing an olive-green T-shirt. "Watch out for the city workers. They just put up a sign over there saying dogs have to be leashed. Apparently they don't want us here. Alfie peed on it."

Wesley checked on Momo. He was still after the white dog.

"There's a lady collecting signatures for a petition to get the city to turn one of these areas into a dog park. You'll see her with her labradoodle. The corner park up the street would be perfect. It's practically unusable right now because of all the homeless people that camp there."

"Kicking out the homeless for a dog park?"

He clicked his tongue. "There are a ton of different places for them to go. Plus, what's happening in that park is not good. The amount of human shit alone. They need to either close it or do something else with it."

Wesley lost sight of Momo and called for him until he came running up from the bottom of the hill trailing the white dog, both with their tongues out. As he leashed the Aussie, a white Ford pickup drove up the cement path and out jumped a woman in uniform. "Ranger!" someone called out. The owners scrambled to grab their animals. Wesley pulled Momo down the hill away from the park. The ranger addressed the owners, "You all wouldn't have to run away if you just kept them on their leashes!" Someone yelled back, "Then give us a dog park!"

Momo strutted down the sidewalk oblivious, panting, content, finding bushes to sniff and pee on.

He posted a close-up picture of the dog's face with the caption:

This one's special. And I mean that in the best possible way. He's got the two-colored eyes. The fuzzy butt. Tons of energy. He's not fantastic on the leash, but he's small enough—get him wet and he'll disappear—he's easy to control. He'd require a yard with adequate space to get his zoomies going. Great dog for a family with kids. If you don't adopt him I probably will. #dogstagram #aussies #wesleyswalks

The post received 97 likes with comments "what a

sweet fur baby!" and "I need this dog in my life" and "100% FLOOF!!!♥♥♥"

25

Henry sat at the desk in his room and wrote a list in his notebook that read:

Why I Should Go Full-time Freelance

- You'll finally have enough time to write what you've wanted to write.
- You won't have a boss.
- You can give yourself good assignments and do meaningful work.
- You'll get bylines in major publications.
- You'll build your resume until you get your dream staff job. Then you'll have the healthcare you need and can save for retirement.
- You may be completely deluded, but why not try?

Over the course of a few days, he pitched all the sites he knew. Magazines and websites in New York, a few in Los Angeles. A lot of his ideas were centered around personal essays about his time abroad, but he was unknown to the coastal editors he contacted, so few were accepted.

For lunch, he stopped at a taco shop for a plate of carnitas. He picked up a copy of the local alt-weekly and paged through the Help Wanted ads. There weren't any journalism jobs. But one of the biggest stories in America was right there in the back of the paper, in the ads for weed so cheap ounces of flower were selling for less than $50.

He saw a job posting for Taylor and Danielle's shop, Sugar Magnolia, and he remembered their offer. The ad read:

Budtenders wanted

Fastest-growing retail marijuana company in Denver seeks knowledgeable, reliable sales associates. Better benefits than other dispensaries. Must be badged and willing to work full-time. Serious inquiries only. Those looking to get high on our supply need not apply.

Send your resume to Wesley Stone: *wesley@sugarmagnolia.com*.

Henry went through the process of getting badged by the Colorado Department of Revenue, then he emailed his resume to Wesley and CC'd Taylor and Danielle. He also shot them both a text saying he'd applied.

Oh we'll hire you, Danielle texted back. *But let's go through the process with Wesley, just so everyone's on the same page.*

Taylor reacted by "emphasizing" his text with two exclamation points.

Wesley emailed back less than an hour later.

Hi Henry,
Taylor told me you're a friend looking for work. No problem. But you're overqualified to work as a budtender. Why would you want to work for us?

Hi Wesley,
Thanks for getting back to me. You're in an expanding industry, and my career field isn't exactly thriving. I'm hoping after I prove myself as a budtender and loyal employee you'll find a way to use my journalism skills to benefit your company.

All right. I'll bite. Come by the office at 2 on Monday.

Henry went to Target and bought a light blue button-down oxford shirt, gray tie, brown belt, navy chinos, and brown desert boots. He tracked the address on his phone, and as soon as the Uber turned down the street near the office he felt overdressed. The building was in an industrial district west of the interstate. It sat among a row of identical flat-topped, brick, single-story warehouses. He detected the musty scent of cannabis before he stepped out of the car. He pulled off the tie and stuffed it in his back pocket.

He rang the buzzer next to the steel door and after a minute a bearded young man opened it. He asked Henry to sign in and handed him a lanyard with a laminated visitor pass to wear around his neck. Henry took a seat in a low, fake leather chair in the foyer. As he waited he noticed the inspirational signs hanging on the walls—IF NOT NOW, WHEN? and IF YOU DON'T HAVE TIME TO DO IT RIGHT, WHEN WILL YOU HAVE TIME TO DO IT OVER? and MAKE TODAY YOUR B*TCH. Employees in street clothes, the trimming and cultivation crew, checked in at the front desk, received their assignments, and disappeared into the warehouse.

After a few minutes, a skinny man with cold hands and a tired smile asked Henry to follow him to his office. Henry sat down and Wesley stared at him across his desk for what felt like an entire minute. Wesley turned and started tapping on his keyboard and looking at his monitor.

"If you're busy I can let you work," Henry said.

"No, just had to send off a quick email. So. What do you know about our company?"

"I've known Taylor and Danielle a long time. I was out of the country when this all started, but I've been following it. And your stores come highly recommended online."

"What are people saying?"

"That you have the best-priced weed that's decent quality."

"Our goal is to become the largest retail cannabis chain in Colorado, which I guess at this point would mean one of the largest in the U.S. Eventually we'll have locations across the country."

"Sounds ambitious."

"The most aggressive plan in the industry. You'll see if we hire you. And I can already tell we're going to offer you a job. But again, I have to ask, aren't you a little overqualified?"

"Maybe at some point you can use my other skills. I could do a good job with marketing or PR. But I'm fine with starting at the bottom. Learning how everything works."

"We definitely could use some help on the marketing front. We're trying to work out the budget for it right now. But yeah, you should know the business first. Come back tomorrow and we'll start your training."

On Day One at Sugar Magnolia, Henry sat on a plastic chair at a spot around a conference table in the cultivation warehouse, which doubled as headquarters. Wesley was holding a meeting for the retail workers—the budtenders—to get them up to speed on new products and sales initiatives. Henry's new coworkers dressed differently than the journalists he was used to. The journos wore shabby business casual—fast-fashion chinos and rumpled collared shirts, well-loved dresses, etc. The budtenders at the table sported stoner street wear—jeans and T-shirts and hoodies, tattoos and piercings on full display, heavy on the personal expression and light on the corporate influence. The dress code was there was no dress code, except the growers had to wear hairnets.

Wesley stood at the head of the table clicking through a PowerPoint presentation on a monitor. He gave context to slides about sales goals for the team with incentives such as cash bonuses for budtenders who upsold products, added commissions for selling certain brands, and a heavy emphasis on moving ounces of flower grown in-house.

"Our goal is to be known for having the cheapest, decent-quality bud in town," Wesley said to the room. "And I'm only going to say this once, so pay attention—we don't limit how much customers can buy in a day. Per transaction, sure. But if someone wants to go out to their car then come back and grab another ounce."

Wesley went through the presentation with an affectation so controlled and practiced it was clear he had rehearsed. Another slide detailed the blanket program—a customer who brought in a blanket for the homeless would receive a 10-percent discount on a Sugar Magnolia-grown ounce. He also explained that he wanted the budtenders to put a card in each shopping bag. The card read:

Sugar Magnolia cannot monitor how much cannabis each individual customer purchases in one day, but we encourage you to comply with state law. Purchase responsibly, enjoy responsibly, and always remember to tip your budtender.

The meeting ended with a slide showing Wesley's vision for Sugar Magnolia, with several additional stores in Colorado, then in five years one in every U.S. state with a recreational marijuana program. Beyond that, in ten years, hopefully with federal cannabis legalization, locations all over the map. The Starbucks of weed. He took a couple of questions—one about how to react to an armed robbery (we'll have more training on that later, he said) and another about proper procedure for storing cash in the vault prior to a pick up. Wesley said he would email Henry some basic FAQs so he could study that night and would be prepared for basic conversations with customers.

When the meeting was over Henry wished he had turned on the recording app on his phone. This was the first instance of what he saw as usable material. When he got on his bike he popped in his bluetooth earbuds and hit record on his app and talked to his phone as he rode home, trying to recall what Wesley had said.

The next day Henry rode to work in a T-shirt and gym shorts. It was the middle of August and the city was thriving with life and noise. The heat from the bike lane radiated up against his legs. He tried not to push his pace too fast—didn't want to show up at work all sweaty.

He locked his bike on the street and went in and found an open locker and took his clothes out of his messenger bag. He changed into a red plaid shirt with pearl snaps and blue jeans. He went out to the sales floor and took a spot behind the counter. Two other budtenders were there on their phones.

The manager's name was Dean. He was stocky, with his dark hair shaved close on the sides and left long on top. He had an outline of Mother England tattooed on his forearm with a dagger where he was born, some city in the south that ended in an X. On the other arm was an insignia of a rugby team he used to play for back home. One of the first things he said to Henry: "That shirt's a little too farmer plaid. We're supposed to be budtenders. Not rednecks."

"I'm sure it'll be fine."

"Up to you, but we're selling weed, not feeding cattle."

One budtender, medium-height with black hair parted left of center and half of it dyed blue, toned shoulders under a white tank top, said, "Oh c'mon, Dean. I'm sure the customers want to see a cowboy. At least he took a shower today."

"Fine, Kat, you like this guy so much, you train him."

For the first half of the day, Henry followed Kat around as she explained to him what to do. She taught him where the products were in the touchscreen point-of-sale system, where to find items stored in the vault, how to work the cash drawer, what to say to customers when they came in. She was a patient teacher and after a couple of hours Henry had a solid understanding. She smelled good and looked fit. After half a day she had him man his own station.

Midway through the afternoon, when he was rushing back to the vault to grab a package of edible chocolate bars, they passed each other and she gave him a smirk. "Stop trying so hard," she said.

At closing time, Henry was trailing Kat to learn all of his end-of-shift duties. She said, "I like your hustle. You'll fit in here if you keep working like that."

"I'm just running around because I don't know what I'm doing."

"Hey, farmer boy!" Dean was at the door by the alley. "Come back here. Got something for you."

Henry went out and Dean stood in a circle with two of the other budtenders. Dean tossed him a Coors Light. "I'm sure you drink this piss where you're from." Dean turned his can, stabbed it with his keys in the side near the bottom, then popped the top and drank from the jagged hole, draining the beer in seconds and dropping the can on the ground.

Henry went through the same actions, coughing at the end.

"I knew this redneck would at least know how to shotgun a beer," Dean said. "Cheers to surviving your first shift."

When Henry went back in, Kat was packing up. She seemed young to Henry, a few years out of college. She accented the outside edges of her eyes with black eyeliner that swept up and made her look like a bird. Henry caught the top of a tattoo on her back. Part of a white crane, backdropped in purple and green. He asked her where she was from.

"Los Angeles."

"No, what country, what nationality?"

"China," she said.

"Ni-hao ma," he said.

"Wow," she said, and laughed. "You're pretty happy with yourself."

The other words he knew were "xie xie," and, "bu ku shay," so he said those, knowing he sounded like an infant.

"So you're a traveler," she asked. "How'd you end up here?"

"I wanted to come back and travel the U.S. This was a good place to start. I don't think I could ever write with real depth or significance if I stayed in Asia. I didn't know the culture or the people well enough."

"Makes sense," she said.

"I loved China. I lived on beer and dumplings the whole month I was there."

"Not a bad diet. OK. Gotta get home," she said. "Take the menus with you. Try to study them. That's what I did."

Henry biked away from the store on tired legs and sore feet. That beer in the alley had only made him want another. He had some cash in his pocket from the shared tips. He had worked his first shift at a new job in a new city. He wanted to celebrate. He went into the first open place he saw, sat down, put the cash on the bar, and drank until the money was gone.

The next day he woke up thinking about Kat. He wasn't scheduled until the following day, so he called Planned Parenthood and asked if they could get him in to have the molluscum removed. They had a cancellation and could fit him in, so he biked over and an old, grumpy nurse froze off the spots. Flat welts remained, but they weren't noticeable.

26.

____

Light came in through the slats of the white blinds on the south-facing window, striping the gray laminate wood floor. Taylor set the kettle on and the clicks from the gas range echoed in the quiet kitchen. She ground coffee, the abrasive noise helping to wake her up. As the coffee brewed in the French press she sat at the table and read her email. Most of it was job ads and newsletters she had signed up for but never read. Then one got her attention.

Subject: hey there

coming to your city! heard good things about that new music venue and an interactive art museum. call me

And with that she was back in Montana with him. Ben. When he was doing "hashtag van life." They had met in Missoula for a weekend of AirBnB sex, coffee, drives out to the country on the dirt roads, stopping to take sunset pictures, dive bars where they played pool and sang along to Bon Jovi on the jukebox, a steakhouse where the conversation turned serious and they told each other they loved one another, another hotel and a hot tub, a bookstore, and against a tree on a secluded path in a park. The rendezvous was only supposed to be two nights, but there was a blizzard and it turned into four.

The blizzard didn't last forever and eventually he went back on the road, to New York and farther, to Brazil, where he was offered a job as a content marketer for an outdoor clothing brand, and he couldn't pass up the chance for fresh photos to post on Instagram. So he left her there, and she let him go.

He'd kept in touch through email and DMs. He was making decisions based on what would be good for him as a content creator—his term for what he did. Traveling enough to fill his passport so full of stamps he needed more pages sewn in. She had to admit he did have a lot of followers on social media.

Taylor was reluctant to meet him. For one, she didn't want him posting about her. He couldn't go out without tagging the people he was with. He hadn't regained enough trust for her to allow that. Also, she wanted another beginning with someone new, someone who hadn't turned his back on her.

Later that day, Taylor was about halfway through a Peloton workout when thoughts of him overwhelmed her. This time from the beginning. He had first entered her life through her phone. A friend had reposted a caption he had written on Instagram and she went through his pictures and found him interesting. So she followed him. He posted a picture a few days later in a blue suit and he was tan and had good posture, nice shoulders, and she commented, "You should always wear a suit." He moved the conversation to their DMs, sending a heart. That's how it had all started.

She was in Denver and he was going to school at the University of Colorado. She finally met him in person at a book launch with a bunch of other social media influencers at a bookstore in Boulder. He had published a collection of what he called essays and poetry, but they were just Instagram captions. He read from a long one about living in San Diego. It wasn't a crowd favorite. Some people left as he read. Others looked at their phones. But she came over to him—he was sitting with the two other writers drinking their one free beer—and said hello.

That summer, he got a job as a waiter at a barbecue restaurant in Estes Park. Taylor stopped in for a drink and he posted about it. The next winter he came home for a funeral and she picked him up at the airport.

They weren't in love until the summer after he graduated college. He decided to spend a few months trying to reconnect with America by buying a cheap van and living out of the back. They had met in Moab, where she was staying with some friends out in the Cowboy Campground, and she invited him to join them. He sat quietly by the campfire listening to them talk about indie music as though it was the most important thing on earth. They made love in his van. She wasn't too impressed. She could tell it wasn't his first time—he knew how to maneuver in that space. Still she went with him to Bryce and Zion, and it was that new-love excitement. They had a lot to talk about, mostly bringing their internet selves to life, asking each other all the questions they had built up about stuff they'd seen online over the years. She also enjoyed it when he would take a cute picture of her and put it on Instagram and it would get hundreds of likes and dozens of comments. She only asked him to let her see the pictures if he was going to post her face.

She stayed with him across Montana and into Washington and down the coast of Oregon. When they got to Southern California her mom called and said she had uterine cancer. Stage 1, scary enough that Taylor flew home and told Ben to come find her in Colorado. Instead, he stayed on the road for a year, trying to get enough material to publish a book about van life.

She had wanted to see him, but she also wanted to start this company. She needed to work on her business application and save money. She decided to let him live his life on the road. She rented a one-bedroom place in Lakewood near a creek. At the time, Danielle was still in Nebraska.

One day, Taylor got a phone call. Ben had gotten tired of

the road, he said, and needed a break. Part of it was he needed a place to stay while a mechanic fixed his transmission. When that was done, he parked his van on her street and made some interior improvements—new flooring, wall and ceiling insulation, black-out curtains.

The more time they spent together, the stronger their bond, and after the van's transmission was repaired and he had the cabinets secured he started talking about going back "out there." The city wasn't enough for him. She asked him to stay, saying they could go together once she had her application submitted and she was waiting to hear back on its approval. But that wasn't his plan.

They were in bed the morning he was supposed to leave. He was responding to comments from a couple of photos he'd posted from older trips.

"People will like your posts more if you have someone with you," Taylor said. "Everyone loves a love story."

"Too difficult with another person," he said, thumbing out a pat, overly positive response with three thumbs-up emojis. "I'm too cheap when I'm on the road. Can you eat rice and beans or peanut butter for every meal? Go a week without taking a shower?"

"We'll find rivers. The ocean. I don't mind going on a diet." She sat up to try to get his attention.

"That old van isn't always that much fun to be in, either. I'm constantly anxious it's going to break down. The A/C barely works." He still hadn't put his phone down.

"You're just making excuses now. Fine. Go on your own."

"C'mon. You know what I'm trying to do."

"No, actually I don't." She got up. "You suck. Don't come back here looking for a bed to sleep in. Don't fucking call me." She went into the bathroom and started a shower.

About 30 minutes later she heard his van start out on the street. She didn't watch him leave.

She had to watch from her phone as he met another woman with a similar idea in Sedona, Arizona. This woman also wanted to be an influencer, and she had convinced him to travel through the desert with her. They showed up in her social feeds for a couple of weeks. Silhouettes of naked sunrise yoga and lake views from the open back doors of his van, their feet sticking up from the blankets in the bed. Then she blocked him.

Ben called her once when he had a signal outside of Lake Tahoe, and she answered: "I'm busy."

"Come back out here," he said. "I miss you."

"Doesn't look like you're too lonely. I gotta go."

She wouldn't answer his calls or his texts. He drove to Colorado and went to the last place he had an address for her after she'd left the Lakewood place, an apartment in Boulder with Tibetan prayer flags draped over the balcony. He buzzed her door and the girl who answered said there was no Taylor there.

He called her again and left her a voicemail. He told her where he was, what he wanted, and she called him back and said she was with someone else.

"You let me get away," she said.

"Fuck," he said. "Are you sure?"

At that point, she wasn't mad at him anymore, so she unblocked him on social media. She had to admit he was pretty damn good at it. He'd post pictures of his dog and how he moved to Iowa for grad school. He almost died when he forgot to set the brake on a moving truck and it rolled down the driveway of his house in Iowa City. He tried to jump in to stop it and got his leg caught under the truck. That content got him a lot of sympathy and engagement.

Then he married a girl who looked a lot like him. Had the same wide mouth and straight smile, bright teeth and a good chin. And with that her access to him went away. Out of respect for his happiness, she wouldn't email him or call him in a moment of weakness.

Cruel life. She had loved him. Now he was out in the world and she'd never see or talk to him again. But she had the business to distract her. He had come to personify all she mourned about her former self. A proxy for what she gave up when decided to get serious about her career.

She carried these feelings for him with her, and at times they came to the surface as a symptom of her unhappiness and anxiety. She talked about him with her mom. When she was drunk and vulnerable she would tell Danielle how she wished she could stop thinking about him. It went on and on and she was frustrated and disappointed with herself. She told herself most people probably had someone like this in their lives, the one person who was perfect that didn't work out. People say things like bad timing, different paths. Divergent interests at that particular time in their lives. No comfort during those nights alone. When she chafed against American culture she thought of her free life, how she had been most free with him.

After she got off the bike, she was alone in a quiet room with a phone next to her and a laptop on the desk. She resisted looking him up online, or worse, responding to his email. A clean break, at least in theory.

He sent a disappointed email afterward. But his visit had sparked his memory enough to write an essay-length Instagram caption under a picture of the tree from their trip to Missoula describing what they did along with some other secrets she had confided in him. He hashtagged it #laterlatergram. She was offended and wrote him a righteously angry email, then unfriended him on all social media. He told her he was sorry and took the post down, but she didn't respond.

A week later she got an email that said: *Your contact Ben Morley is on LinkedIn*, with a blue CONNECT button. Her feelings finally started to change. His headshot made him look older, with less hair, and he seemed happy, but in a professional way. He wore a trimmed beard now. Not as youthfully handsome as she remembered, but how could he be? He was dressed in a suit, a professional headshot, and smiled confidently into the camera. She looked through his resume, seeing what he had accomplished since they had split, and she knew he was fine without her. An upward career trajecto-ry. Probably a good salary, health insurance, a 401k. *That* was what she needed to move on. She deleted the LinkedIn email and went outside.

27

Danielle ordered a shot of whiskey and a Budweiser. There was a guy in the front sitting at the rack who reminded Danielle of Henry. The dancer was laughing at his jokes, teasing him, and out came his wallet. The guy stacked up ten singles and the dancer took his cap and wore it backward as she used her moves to suck up the money. As soon as her act was over, she was out on the floor and she only had to say a sentence or two before the guy agreed to follow her to a private room.

Danielle turned back to the bar and took out her phone. She wanted to text Flannery: *are you dancing tonight?* But she decided not to send it.

She was reading through work emails when she felt a hand on her back. It was her. Wearing a silver wig and purple lipstick. "Hey," she said, with the corner of her mouth turned up. "Funny running into you here."

"Hey," Danielle said. "What—?"

"Can't really chat. I'm on next."

Danielle tried to act like she was looking at her phone while Flannery worked through her set. After she finished her songs, Dani watched to see if she would try to work the floor, but she didn't come out, so Danielle found her on the back patio smoking a cigarette with her feet up on a chair. Danielle lit a joint and walked over.

"You can't smoke that out here, honey," Flannery said. "You really are high all the time aren't you?"

Danielle stood in front of her, took a drag then exhaled up into the evening air. "You fucked me up," she said.

Flannery put her feet down. "Baby, you did that all on your own."

Danielle took another drag. Looked at her feet.

"Yep. Get even higher," Flannery said, laughing. "You poor thing. Oh, are you sad? Am I supposed to apologize? How about this? I'll give you a dance for half price then we can just be friends and forget any of this ever happened? You want closure? Twenty bucks is all it'll cost you. I'd give it to you for free, but the club has to get its cut."

"How about you act like you're not working and I'm not a customer."

"Honey, you came to see me at my work. If you don't want a dance you're just costing me money."

"Great. Thanks for making me feel stupid."

"How it is sometimes. You should go home."

"I actually thought this might work out."

"Seriously? Listen. You met Paul. It's too boring to tell you the whole story, but we've been waiting for each other a long time."

"I get that, but why didn't you tell me that when I met you?"

"Oh I can't do this. You're acting just like every other dickhead guy who comes in here. You think you bought my affection. For some reason, I thought because you were ... that you'd be smarter than them."

Danielle took a step closer. "Did you just call me stupid? Fuck you, bitch."

"Nope. You can't talk to me like that here." Flannery said the last part loud enough that one of the bouncers noticed and moved toward them.

Danielle dropped her lit joint into Flannery's drink and went back in and sat at the stage. The bouncer spoke with

Flannery then followed her in. She was rummaging in her purse for a few dollar bills when he caught up with her and said, "All right. Time to go, sweetheart."

He held out his hand to help her up.

As she walked out she turned to the bouncer and said, "I could say a lot of things you'd have trouble dealing with right now."

"Don't come back," he said.

She stepped out under the humming neon lights to another indifferent city, a city of people and places where she meant nothing and that meant nothing to her. The sky was cloudless and plain. The sidewalk felt cold and hard and all she could hear was the little insignificant tapping of her feet as she walked away from the club.

28.

At the pre-staff meeting, Henry stood at the back of the store as Dean went over the promotions and changes to the menu. Blue Dream and Gorilla Glue were sold out. Grandpa's Breath was half price. Henry wore a black shirt with pearl snap buttons and jeans. As the meeting broke up, Dean said to Henry, "That shirt's better than the redneck plaid you wore yesterday, but you still look like a fake cowboy."

"And you look like a guy who wishes he were American," Henry said.

"Like hell." Dean squared up to Henry, stocky and short, with his chin up. "I would never call myself one of you lot. I'm only in this disaster of a country temporarily. Now can you please fuck off and stock your counter? And try not to cock it up, please?"

Henry laughed as he went over to set up his station. The store hadn't been open for more than 20 minutes before a group of young women came in. The automated numbering system assigned them to Henry. They were loud, joyful, making each other laugh, dressed for a day out. Henry tried his best to entertain them, smiling, asking them where they were from, what they had going on today.

One woman—with brown curls, a light gray dress, and a gold necklace—asked Henry how long he'd worked there, and if he liked it. As he was saying it was fine, Dean slid over and told Henry to go find more Incredibles from storage, said his station wasn't properly stocked. Henry rolled his eyes and saluted behind Dean's back, winking at the woman. He rushed to the storage room and got the chocolate bars. When he returned, Dean was leaning over the counter with his legs spread far apart and his hands behind his back, in what the other budtenders called the wide stance.

"So those caramel chews?" The woman pointed to the wrapped toffee bars and asked Henry. "How strong are they? Do I just eat the whole thing?"

"Yep," Henry said. "They're delicious."

"Actually that's utterly wrong," Dean said. "If you eat an entire chew you'll have consumed 100 milligrams of THC. You'll be off your tits."

"That's what I meant. Don't eat the whole thing." Henry put his hands together and bowed slightly. "We here at Sugar Magnolia would like you to please stay on your tits."

The woman laughed.

"Can we get you anything else? Not you," Dean said to Henry. "You go away."

Henry was ringing up another patron when the woman with the necklace came back over, slightly breathless. She slid a piece of paper across the counter but was too embarrassed to speak. Henry dumbly said, "OK." She turned and left with a laugh.

Henry buzzed through the rest of his day and his closing duties. He walked out with one of his fellow budtenders, Miles, to a nearby bar that claimed to be Irish where a lot of the service industry people hung out after work. Miles was wearing a red cap with a long bill and a short-sleeved, white collared shirt with a pineapple pattern. He had been working at Sugar Magnolia for a few months, and Henry noticed his coworkers liked him. He'd already charmed several of the female budtenders. He had a reputation Henry didn't understand. He talked in a way that sounded brilliant, but Henry never really got his jokes.

As they made their way to the bar, Miles said he had an MFA in creative writing from Hunter College in New York. He said one of his best friends, a guy in his cohort, was on some 30 under 30 list of best young writers in the country, and Miles couldn't get published anywhere. "Don't even try it," he told Henry, shaking a preroll out of a white plastic tube and lighting it as they walked down the street. "It's not worth it."

They had barely sat down at the bar when Miles ordered a shot of Jameson and a Coors Light.

"This fucking 21st century, man. I hate that I was born in this era." He took the shot of whiskey. "Look at how I'm fucking dressed. I look like I'm 10 years old."

A beautiful Latina woman walked by in jean shorts and a white linen button-up shirt.

"Fffff. This bar," Miles said. He leaned back on his stool and drank a third of his beer. "This fucking city. I always imagined myself dying on some great battlefield somewhere."

"Where'd that come from?" Henry asked.

"Bob Dylan."

Miles ordered another round of Jameson shots then opened his arms and spun around and rested his back against the bar. "Look at these hipsters. All this irony. We're all in on the joke. I could've been great if I was born a hundred years ago."

"You told me last time we hung out that you had lived in New York. You saw all the people trying as hard as they could to be good at the city. Not good at what they do. Just good at the city."

Henry peeled the label off of his bottle.

"Fuck, I don't know," Miles said. "I want to write, but I don't want to write shit. The world is full of mediocrity. A lot of people need to be told that what they're doing isn't good enough and they're never going to make it. I'm 35 years old and I haven't published a word, haven't even *finished* anything. I thought I'd at least have my first book done by now. You know how much work it takes to write a book? How many times you have to say no to your friends? To the girl you want to sleep with? We're all talented; we wouldn't be trying if we weren't. But talent means nothing without discipline. And there's no way to be disciplined and still know what's going on out there."

"Then just do the work, right?" Henry said.

"I know. I know. You can work. You're a Midwestern guy who can buck hay. I've heard your farm stories."

"Maybe you should quit," Henry said. "It'll probably make you feel better."

"That's pretty harsh."

"Do it. Quit. I'm serious. Quit and you'll never be tortured by it again. I gave up playing guitar. I couldn't do it. I'm not going to be a songwriter. I know that. Now I have more time to do other things. Like sitting around wishing I was born in the 1800s so I could be Doc Holliday, or Buffalo Bill, or whoever it is you think you'd be better off being."

"You know what, man? You're a condescending dick. You're not that much younger than me. What have you written? Some shitty small town journalism? Some shit for an Asian newspaper no one gives a fuck about? A novel you claim almost got published, but no one knows if that's true? And just because you say it's good doesn't mean it's good. You want the life of a writer so much you'll say anything to get closer to it."

"All right," Henry said, smiling. "Now we're getting somewhere."

"Maybe this is all bullshit. Maybe we all think we're going to be the next Beat Generation. When really we're just a lost generation. And not *the* Lost Generation. There are probably a dozen houses in this city right now with people sitting in their living rooms dreaming about being writers or musicians or painters. If they're not staring at a screen... But why? Nobody cares. Everyone wants art but no one wants to make it. And this country doesn't give a fuck about its artists."

"Yep. Agreed. 100 percent. But at least if you do something, if you make something, you're not a poser, or a leech. There are probably hundreds of people writing right now, too, people creating all across this city. They're getting ahead. Doing the real work."

They were both getting drunk. Miles' posture was suffering, his neck and shoulders leaning forward, and Henry had an acidic, metallic taste in his mouth.

"Fuck it, man," Henry said. "I'm going home, to bed. I do want to work in the morning."

"You do that. Thanks for making me feel like shit. Helluva pep talk."

Henry was wobbly getting on his bike, but after he picked up speed he went straight down the sidestreets, coasted through stop signs, smiled at the girls on the sidewalks, and sang "Tangled Up in Blue" in a low voice, mumbling through the lines he didn't know.

The next day he woke up too hungover to write, so he got ready for work by drinking black tea and doing pushups. At the pre-shift meeting, he was tired and his legs were sore. Dean brought up the group of women, explaining how Henry could have steered them wrong and one of them would have had a bad experience from eating too much of an edible.

"It's very good I was there," Dean said. "They ended up buying a couple hundred dollars worth of product. Tipped well, too. No thanks to this wanker."

"Did you get a number, too?" Henry reached in his back pocket, pulled out the paper, and read, "'Cassie. Call me.' She seems nice."

"Unbelievable. She gave this tosser her number after he told her to eat the entire edible. Probably would've ended up in hospital."

Two days later, Wesley came to the store to check on inventory. He stood at the back and observed with Dean at his side. He noticed how Henry was hustling from his station back to the stockroom to grab more paraphernalia and smiling as he interacted with his customer. "He seems into it."

Dean said, "Yeah, that guy. Could've given him a miss. He's what the kids call a try-hard."

When Henry rushed back, Wesley stopped him and asked, "Hey, do you have any siblings or cousins back on the farm who want jobs?"

Dean's face dropped. Henry laughed and went on with this work. But throughout the day he considered what his family would think. The men in his father's generation would not be proud of him working for some other business owner, unless he was learning how to run his own business, but that wasn't the case. He thought about calling home and what he would say. "Just got a job in the marijuana industry to make some cash while I look for better work." Not the strongest position. He'd try to wait to call home until he had better news about a real job.

At the end of the shift, no one was shotgunning beers or doing much at all. They had been busy with repeat customers buying ounce after ounce and everyone looked tired. The staff split tips and dispersed into the night. Henry went to the bar next door and sat on a stool and scrolled through his Instagram feed. Several of his friends who were still in Asia posted their travel photos of beaches in Thailand and ramen in Japan and nightlife in Singapore.

"So did you call Carrie or whatever her name was?" Kat said as she sat down. She was wearing a blue hairband and a white halter top with dark brown jean shorts. Black flip flops. Her skin summer tan and radiant.

"Cassie. Not yet," Henry said. "I just got her number. Trying to play it cool."

"But you are going to call her," she said.

"Might shoot her a text." Henry locked his phone and set it down.

"So half a phone call then."

"Don't want to come on too strong."

"Men are dumb."

"What if I said you look nice in this light? Is that dumb?"

"100% dumb. Too cheesy."

"But true though."

"Fine. I'll take it."

The bartender, Jim, caught the last part of that exchange as he muddled mint for a mojito nearby. "Shit, Kat," he said. "What are you doing? Look at that shit-eating grin. You're too smart for that."

"Aww, Jim. You're sweet." She looked at Henry and rolled her eyes. "What do you think about going for a bike ride?"

"Either that or I have to fight this guy."

Jim snorted as he worked his way down the bar with a wet rag.

"Nah, don't worry about him. He shot his shot—he missed."

They rode down the middle of the street, the city night air cool and dry. They chatted as they went, Kat talking about work and telling Henry what she thought of all the personalities. Who to be friends with, who to stay away from. Henry laughed at the way she described people and the impressions she did. She nailed Dean's accent, for one.

At a park, they took a path that wound down to a lake ringed by pine trees. They stopped by a row of adjustable lounge chairs and laid their bikes in the grass. Kat had a metal flask in her pack that she took a drink from and handed to Henry. It was cinnamon whiskey, warm and sweet.

"Can I call you Hank? I like that name."

"I'm not opposed to that. My mom is the only one who insists on calling me Henry. She says she didn't name me one thing so people could call me something else."

A few geese paddle across the lake, v-shaped ripples forming on the surface.

"Can I ask you something?" Hank asked.

"Sure."

"Are you single?"

She leaned over and kissed him—the cinnamon whiskey again. He pulled the stand out from the back of her chair to make it flat. He took off his shirt. He tried to take off hers but she said no. She did let him take her leggings off. The park was dark and quiet around them. "This is nice," Kat said. They were rushed and the sex would've been better if they knew each other well.

They dressed quickly and Kat broke the silence. "My legs are shaking," she said. Hank took another drink from the flask then grabbed her bike and brought it to her. They rode to the stoplight and he made to follow her.

"I'm actually that way and you're that way," she said.

"Thanks. Got a little turned around."

She kissed him on the cheek and said, "Call me whenever. And don't be weird at work."

29

Taylor slept in fits. She'd had a nightmare about her teeth falling out, and Louie kept coming in the room and whimpering. His cancer was progressing, and he couldn't see very well anymore. The CBD oil she had been putting on his food wasn't helping. She needed to make a decision but she didn't want to make it.

She drank two cups of coffee at home, but she was still tired and behind schedule when she drove to the office and hustled into a meeting Wesley was leading.

"You were late, so I went ahead and got started," Wesley said. He sat at one end of the conference table, passing his fingers over the laptop trackpad. He found the graphic he wanted and shared his screen on the monitor. The line graph showed sales by type of product—edibles, concentrates, pre-rolls, flower, vape cartridges, and other infused products. Each category was a small column except for flower, which towered above the others.

"We're moving pounds of bud out the door," he said. "The blanket program has been a success. If we keep this up we should be in good shape. No one else is being this aggressive."

"How confident are we this is compliant?" Taylor asked.

"I consulted with Haviletsky."

"And he said this was fine? 100 percent legit?"

"Well, he said the language in the regulations is vague. That we weren't clearly breaking any laws."

"That doesn't sound definitive," Taylor said. She looked to Danielle for assurance, but Dani was staring up at the screen.

"These sales numbers seem solid to me," Danielle said.

"I just don't want to jeopardize our license," Taylor said.

"This is how we bring in revenue," Wesley said. "We have to keep pushing it."

"OK, thanks, Wesley," Taylor said. "Do you have anything else?"

"Nope. Just to say this is working."

"Would you mind giving us the room?"

"No problem."

Taylor waited until he closed his laptop and left. She turned to Danielle and said, "This feels risky."

"I don't know. It seems to be working. This is what we hired him for, right?"

"What if we're breaking the law? You can find a lawyer to say anything you want if you ask enough lawyers."

"I say we see how it plays out."

Back in her office, Taylor turned on the electric kettle for tea and drafted an email:

Subject: Wesley's plan

I've made my objections clear about this. Let's figure out a compromise here. It's risky. Maybe too risky.

T.

She paused before clicking send. She reread the email one more time, feeling her heart rate jump. They couldn't allow this guy to burn their business to the ground. She sent it.

"Hey, do you have a minute?" Taylor said from the doorway of Danielle's office. Danielle glanced at her, finished typing. Taylor waited. "If you're busy I can come back."

"No, come in. Sit down." Danielle turned to face her. The inside corners of her eyes were dark.

Taylor closed the door as Danielle shut her laptop.

"I sent you an email about this, but I thought we should talk." Taylor took a breath. "When we agreed to start this business, I did it because I trusted you."

"I feel like there's a 'but' coming here."

"I still trust you. I also think we might be making the wrong move."

"The growth strategy."

"That, my dumb idea with the van, this whole thing in general. But also Wesley. We're giving him a lot of say in how we run our business." She waited for Danielle to speak, but Dani let the pause hang in the air. "I think he only cares about making as much money as he can."

"Which we're not opposed to, are we? Early retirement sounds pretty nice. Exit plan and all that. Are you getting scared?"

"I'm not scared. Just trying to be smart."

"And we're not being smart?"

"That's not what I meant. All I'm saying is either we reel this back in and try to grow our company legally or—"

"Or what? You can say it."

"Or I might be out."

"We're making money. I don't see the problem."

"Think about it. That's all I'm asking."

Taylor walked out of the office and out to her SUV, relieved she had spoken her mind. In her car, she turned on Colorado Public Radio. The radio hosts were talking about Russia. Her clothes reeked of raw cannabis, skunky, like diesel fuel.

She went home and worked out in the basement. Yoga, pilates, bodyweight exercises. She was eating delivery Thai food when Danielle came in.

"Something smells amazing," Danielle said, setting her bag onto the couch.

Taylor opened a bottle of Sauvignon Blanc and poured two glasses.

"Can I talk to you?" she asked.

"Of course." Danielle sat on a stool at the island.

"When we started this I said I don't want this business to fuck up our friendship."

Danielle took a sip of her wine. "I remember, and I agree."

"So how do we make sure we don't let money fuck it up?"

"Look, I'm all in on this," Danielle said. "You. Me. The business. We just need to see it through. Our plan has always been to build it up until we get bought out. I say we stick to that."

"You think this is going to work?"

"I do. There's no going back at this point. We're too invested."

"OK. Yeah. Sure."

"Hey, c'mon. We're killing it. You saw the numbers. We gotta ride it out. Until they really make this shit legal, we're all breaking the law anyway. We need to get paid. And we will."

"I saved you some of this," Taylor said, sliding over the pad see ew. Danielle picked up a thick noodle with chopsticks.

Taylor sat back and watched her eat.

30

Henry was on break, leaning his back against the building in the alley behind the store, when he texted the woman from the other day, Cassie. He wrote he was the budtender she met at Sugar Magnolia and they should get together if she was still in town. She responded with omg. He waited for her to elaborate, but she never did.

He went back to work and kept his attention on Kat. He figured if he wasn't going to travel from place to place looking for short-lived, intense interactions with strangers, then he might as well try to build a life with the people he met here. As he finished his end-of-shift work, he stopped her as she walked by and asked, "Meet you next door?"

"Order me a shot and a beer in exactly twelve minutes," she said.

Henry took his products from the counter and put them in the vault. The shift had been busy—they had run out of several strains of flower up front. He counted his tips. Not terrible.

In exactly twelve minutes, Kat slid onto the stool next to him, picked up her shot and clinked it against his and they drank them together. They faced forward, analyzing the bottles and taps and decorations as Jim worked.

Jim made them a free drink, some cocktail he was developing, in exchange for their feedback. "He's still trying with you," Henry said. Kat pretended to gag herself with her fingers down her throat and said the drink tasted like flowers, lime juice, and gym socks. Jim poured them small glasses of leftover punch.

Henry learned Kat had been looking into going to Prague to teach English, and she wanted his advice. She was a "secret writer like him"—her words —turning 30 soon, and she said she felt like her youth was escaping her.

She said she understood how it felt to live in the States after time abroad. In college, she'd had a scholarship at Oxford in England, and when the semester ended she'd decided to stay. That turned into two more years in Europe. But she'd been back in the U.S. longer than Henry and felt like it was time to leave again.

When the bar closed, Henry suggested they rent scooters. Kat said she was up for it. They paid their tabs and walked to the bus stop where three white and green electric scooters leaned on a sidewalk bench. They each had the app on their phones so they activated the pair with the most battery life. They pushed off and rode down the sidewalk, east through the city. The plastic wheels clattered on the sidewalk joints as they passed the mansions and apartment buildings, under the branches of the hundred-year-old trees, the night air cool on their faces. There was laughter and whooping as they dodged obstacles and people walking with their pets. Henry rode with his right foot against the back fender and leaned into the turns to avoid trash and places where tree roots buckled the pavers. They passed the Queen Anne Victorian houses with fish scales in the gables that cost millions of dollars. Owning that home would require a time machine set for 1970.

Kat turned around to smile back at him, and as he waved back he veered off the sidewalk into a grass patch. The scooter stopped, but he kept going and landed on the lawn. Kat came back laughing. "I'm dead," he said.

She gave him a hand, and they continued on until they stopped at a light. Henry leaned over and kissed her.

"The Big Dipper," she said and pointed up.

When the stoplight changed they rode to the park and followed the oval path around to the white pavilion with pillars that could have belonged in ancient Greece. They set the scooters aside and walked toward a cluster of oak trees. Kat went to a low tree branch, wrapped her arms around it, swung her leg over and hoisted herself up another branch. "You coming?" she asked.

Henry shook his head then reached up and pulled himself up onto the low branch. The movement tweaked his back but not bad enough that he couldn't keep going. They climbed until the limbs thinned out and were too skinny to support their weight.

"Did you know this used to be a cemetery?" Henry said. "Imagine how many ghosts are out here."

They looked out, listening to a siren fade off into the night.

"You think you'll leave again?" Kat asked.

"Probably. I wish I could say I'd be happy with just traveling overseas once a year or something. But I don't know. I mean, Mother America keeps you close. Under her wing. Hard to leave once you're back."

"True."

"But how lucky are we, really? Sitting here talking about 'traveling,' which is just another word for 'extended vacation.' There are people sleeping under those trees over there."

"There are people under the ground." Kat leaned against the tree trunk. "It's not our fault our generation has been priced out. It used to be a choice. Buy a house if you want one. Have a family. How does anyone do that now if your family doesn't give it to you? The only choice I have is to live out in the world. Keep moving."

"I left the States post-recession, and everyone says we're due for another one. So maybe it'll get cheaper again."

"That's kind of fucked up—to hope for the economy to crash so we can afford a one-bedroom in the city. When was the last time you went home?"

"I can't go home. Broke. No car. Working a pot job. Too embarrassing."

Henry looked west over the houses. The street lights shrunk in size until they became blurry, soft glowing points.

"Same. It's hard to even call home right now. Are you ready to get down? My butt's falling asleep."

They climbed down and picked up their scooters.

"This one's battery's almost dead," Kat said. "two percent."

"Let's double up."

"OK, but I'm driving. My place?"

Henry grabbed Kat tight around the waist and they rode back toward her apartment, the scooter wheels clacking on the pavement, the motor whining softly in the night.

At the store, Henry entered his pass key into the iPad and called up the point-of-sale system. His station at the retail counter was behind a clean glass case. He had the products arranged with the four shelves of flower in descending levels of quality on his right and edibles and concentrates on his left, behind him the vape pen batteries, prerolls, dab rigs and a cooler with cannabis-infused beverages—sodas, non-alcoholic beer, and cold brew coffees.

In a staff meeting earlier that week, Wesley had told the budtenders that when he designed the shop he prided himself on its minimalist aesthetic. This particular location was in a converted warehouse in a formerly industrial neighborhood. Now, the area was mostly breweries, food trucks, and art galleries. The interior of the store was exposed brick walls and ductwork for the heating and cooling system. Sugar Magnolia held a dual license—retail and cultivation—for the space, with a 100-plant grow in the basement. The company spent considerable money on ventilation so the shop didn't make the neighborhood reek of marijuana, but Henry, and the customers, could smell it.

Henry's first customer walked in—a squat, heavy man in a gray T-shirt and black gym shorts. He held up his ticket with a number from the waiting room. Henry checked his ID—47, from Amarillo, Texas. The man asked to buy an ounce of their cheapest flower. Henry took out a plastic container from a drawer beneath the case, logged it in the system, counted the man's $60, which was about as cheap as anywhere in town, bagged the pot, and stapled the receipt to the bag. The guy walked out and Henry waited for his next customer.

Fifteen minutes later, his iPad screen flashed with another number. In walked the same guy from Texas. This time he had an olive green blanket in hand.

"Forgot to bring this in last time. Another ounce."

Henry tossed the blanket into a bin and rang him up with the 10-percent discount, handed him the ounce, and watched him leave. In fifteen minutes he was back. This went on for about two hours. That guy didn't buy all of his ounces from Henry, but Henry noticed each time he came in. If Henry had to guess, he would say the guy bought at least a pound that day. It didn't take much imagination to see he was buying it to resell, probably back in Texas. No one person could smoke that much weed before it went stale. Henry realized the cops or state regulatory officers would view it the same way. This was the beginning of a good story. He made quick notes on the scraps of paper on the counter and shoved them into his back pocket. Tomorrow he'd bring something better to write on.

Kat had mentioned to Henry that budtenders came and went, to not get too attached to anybody, and she was right. Each week a few quit and few more started. Transplants from other parts of the country, the Midwest or the South or somewhere like Massachusetts. Places where the families would come here to vacation and the kids would have fond memories, vowing one day to return to live. The ones who wanted to work for Sugar Magnolia were either cannabis entrepreneur wannabes or stoners looking for a discount. They had no loyalty to any job or employer. Working for the marijuana industry was one stop on the ride they'd tell their friends and family about when they went back home. Many barely lasted a week. The turnover rate was the highest Henry had ever seen of any business he'd been a part of, including the restaurant industry. When he was promoted to assistant store manager after a few weeks he didn't get too proud of himself. He'd simply lasted longer than everyone else, and it helped that he knew the owners.

Henry had no real benefits or health insurance yet, but he did get a slight raise with more responsibilities and duties. He would also be part of a weekly meeting led by Wesley to discuss product selection, marketing and promotions, and their ongoing strategy to become the number one supplier of flower ounces in the state. When the promotion was announced Dean was pissed. He sulked and said exactly one sentence to Henry all day. "Hey farmer boy, go get the broom."

It was against company policy for workers to use their personal phones at the counter while they worked, but there was nothing in the rules saying Henry couldn't keep a notebook next to him. If he had tried to film what went on with his phone, people would be suspicious, but the general public had become so oblivious to the idea that someone might be writing down notes about what they saw or heard on pen and paper that no customers ever asked him about it. He assumed they thought it was somehow related to his duties as store manager.

After work, he went home and processed the notes into a cloud-based document on his laptop. The task was boring administrative work, so he did what he could to make it more interesting. He packed marijuana flower into a handheld vaporizer with a light on the tip that glowed green when he sucked on it. He slipped into a flow with his music on the Bluetooth speaker, typing in rhythm to the songs.

He could tell he had smoked too much when the pot brought to the surface a moment from his past he was ashamed of, a time he had been a coward, for instance, or a pressing, current, unresolved anxiety. How he would probably die alone, broke, and unfulfilled. Failure his biggest anxiety. Mediocrity. Tedium. A life poorly lived. Work alleviated all of that. Accomplishments were the best way to counteract it. But some days it felt like he'd never finish anything, never have the success he wanted. And that night he fixated on that idea, played it over and over in his mind until he was forced to change what he was doing.

He closed his computer and went outside. It was warm and dark and the city pulsed with activity. Car traffic and groups of friends on the sidewalks on their way to bars and houses. He walked with his headphones in, listening to a podcast about how to be a better investigative reporter, how to write stories people cared about, how to do more meaningful work—work he wasn't yet doing but wanted to. He tried to apply what he was learning to what was happening at his job. He could tell the word was getting around that Sugar Magnolia was different. Customers came in and said to him, "I hear you guys don't care how much pot I can buy," or, "I love how I can buy ounces here like it's nothing. Most places don't let you do that," or, "I was reading online that you guys are the place to go to stock up."

He sold a lot of product to tourists and out-of-towners. One guy came into the store from South Dakota and said, "This here shit's way too powerful. I remember when we used to get all our grass from Mexico. Brown weed with seeds. Might pop a little when you put the fire to it. We could smoke all day and be A-OK. This here shit makes me want to piss my pants." But he also sold a lot of flower to people with out-of-state licenses who weren't on vacation. These customers had no questions, weren't curious, had only one objective: They were on a mission to buy as many ounces as they could.

He wrote it all down. The notebook was quickly filling

with snippets of dialogue, character descriptions, and his own analysis of how legal cannabis was playing out and how it was affecting individuals and society. When he got back home from his walk, he began working on a pitch to send to national magazines. He planned to write an undercover look at the inner workings of the industry. He wanted to call it "Cannabis Confidential," and expose the real truth of how the marijuana market was unfolding, with the goal of turning a national magazine story into a full-length, reported, non-fiction book. A story with commercial appeal that could sell.

Henry wasn't sure if it was better to write on spec—to do the piece and see if he could sell it—or pitch first. He tried not to write for free, which was what writing on spec would be if he couldn't sell the story, and he wanted to hold fast to that rule. So he crafted a careful pitch explaining who he was, his platform, what the story was about, how long it would be, and who he would interview. He went online and searched magazines' About Us sections for the email addresses of editors he wanted to pitch, created a spreadsheet to track the submissions, and sent out about a dozen emails. Then he went to the bar on the corner and sat by the taps, drank craft beer, and watched baseball for a couple of hours.

The following week, Henry's pitch was accepted by a slightly left-of-center national magazine that wanted him to write a 3,000-word, reported essay. The message came in on Monday morning as he was checking his email before work. He stood up and paced, looking at the computer, thinking about how to respond. This was the break he wanted, and it was all tenuous. He knew the stakes. He could say the wrong thing and upset the editor. He could botch the assignment. A story like this could crack his freelance career wide open. It might lead to more work and a book deal if the article took off. If he really wanted to make it as a freelancer, he needed to execute as flawlessly as possible—source it thoroughly, nail the word count, meet the deadline. He wouldn't get another chance to make a first impression with this editor and publication.

Before he left for work, he sent Taylor and Danielle an email telling them he had received a freelance story assignment and asked if he could interview one of them. After he arrived at the store, he checked his email and saw Danielle had suggested he interview Wesley. She said he could cut out early from his retail shift to do it that afternoon if he wanted.

Henry prepared by writing questions in his notebook as he worked his half-day shift. He wrote dozens, way more than he would need or have time to ask, but he wanted to make sure he had enough. Nothing worse than running out of things to ask during an interview. He rode over to the warehouse headquarters, the summer heat and light starting to wane. A beautiful, perfect afternoon. He checked in with the front desk receptionist and was told to wait until Wesley would see him. He kept himself occupied by paging through the cannabis trade publications—*Marijuana Industry Monthly*, *Cannabis Economy Executive*—on the coffee table. In nearly all of the photos, people stood in greenhouse rooms full of cannabis plants. The stories were written in a business-to-business style that provided tips and strategies for executives in the industry—quick, to the point, full of "actionable" information.

After waiting for about 15 minutes past their agreed upon time, he walked to Wesley's office. Judging by their smiles and laughter, the owners were having a casual conversation. Henry knocked and they turned and looked at him like what do *you* want? Early on, Taylor and Danielle had warned him they couldn't give him any special treatment just because they were friends. "Let's keep it professional," Taylor had said. But they waved him in.

"Sorry, guys. I have an appointment with Wesley."

"Oh right," Danielle said. "Make us look good."

The two women left and closed the door. Wesley gestured for Henry to sit down across from him.

"That meeting stopped being productive a long time ago," Wesley said. "So how are you liking the job so far?"

"The general public's interesting. And the general cannabis public is another level of interesting."

"I'm sure it's not boring. So, what are we talking about today?"

"The article's about how you've been able to grow the company so effectively. The story behind the rapid growth here. A business profile. But it's about the broader industry, as well."

"Got it."

"Can we start at the beginning? What was the company like when you first came on board? Oh, and before you answer, do you mind if I record?" Wesley shook his head. Henry opened the Voice Memo app on his phone and hit the red button.

"A year ago there were less than 30 employees here. Now we have more than 300."

"Exactly what I want to talk about. How have you been able to achieve such exponential growth in such a short time?"

Henry sat back, attempting to create a relaxed rapport with Wesley, to make him feel comfortable and willing to be candid and open. Wesley provided the summarized version of his backstory. He told Henry an anecdote about his own job interview at Sugar Magnolia, where at the end of the conversation Taylor asked Wesley to write down what he thought he should be paid. "They told me later they would have agreed to a lot more," Wesley said.

"How did they know to contact you?"

"Off the record?"

"Sure."

"I had a reputation. I was working for medical marijuana distributors here before it was fully legal. And before that, in dispensaries in Oakland, California. I know what to do."

Henry did his best to act entertained and genuinely interested in each of Wesley's stories and answers. He listened as closely as he could, not to process everything to memory, but to identify any information that was incomplete or would appear vague on the page. He tried to anticipate an editor asking for more questions or examples, and when he spotted an ambiguous answer he jumped in with a follow-up question. His go-to favorites were, "Help me to understand that a little more," and, "Can we go over that again?" and he also often asked, "What do you mean by that?" or, "Do you have an example of how that might work?"

Henry had carefully avoided not mentioning explicitly what he observed during the day at the store, particularly the same customers coming back multiple times in one day and Sugar Magnolia's reputation for cheap, readily available ounces. But Henry needed more details to flesh out his story, and he needed Wesley to comment on this specific business aspect. He had to ask about the purchase limits and the sales practices.

"Do you think not limiting the amount of flower customers can purchase has had an impact on Sugar Magnolia's success?"

Wesley looked down before he answered.

"Funny you ask that. Our company has intentionally developed a brand reputation for selling low-cost, consistent-quality flower. I've said that a thousand times, but it's a huge part of our marketing strategy."

"And it's working. But no concerns about pushing it too far?"

Wesley paused. Henry thought he might not answer.

"What do you mean by 'too far?'"

"You're on the cutting edge. Going where the competition won't."

"The law's vague on that. We might be driving right up to the line, but we're not going over it."

"That's a good quote."

"That's what my lawyer tells me."

He switched to another line of questioning, asking about

future plans for growth, how many stores the company want-ed to have by the end of next year, plans for expansion to other states, and where Wesley saw the company going in five years. They spoke for about an hour, and with his own day-to-day observations, he had plenty of material for the story. He saved and labeled the voice recording file in his phone then stood up to leave.

"You sure you have what you need?" Wesley asked. "How do you think the story's going to look?"

"Yep. I'm good. A lot of good insights and answers. Thank you."

"Could we read the story before it's published?"

"Against policy. I never allow prior approval."

"Not even for your boss?"

"Best I can do is let you read your quotes. I can send those over when I write it up."

"That would be good."

"Last thing, we'll need some images. Of you. The store. Whatever you have."

"We can get you some pictures. We just had a PR team over here with a camera."

Henry rode home barely seeing the street in front of him. He was crafting the lede and organizing the outline as he rode. He stopped at the convenience store for a bag of pista-chios and a two-liter bottle of Coke Zero.

Before Henry began to write the story he used the tricks he knew to structure it. He transcribed the interview with Wesley, printed it out at the FedEx down the street, then back at his apartment laid out three different colors of high-lighter—yellow, pink, and blue—each shade representing a different section corresponding to a rough outline. He had learned he could save himself time and effort by sketching out the structure and organizing his material before he began the actual writing. His back was still fucked up, but he knew if he took an Oxy he wouldn't be able to write, so he gritted it out—drank the pop and worked through a bowl of nuts, stopping to do the stretches the doctor taught him when it got too painful.

After he highlighted each paragraph, he cut the pieces up and arranged them by color on the floor. He taped them together and consulted the scroll as he retyped the first draft on his computer. He left gaps in the document and notes to himself in brackets where he wanted to fill in descriptions and his own thoughts, impressions, and personal anecdotes.

After he had the draft composed, he took a thumb drive back to FedEx, printed the draft, and with a red pen he wrote in what he had experienced at work, consulting his notebook for details, pieces of dialogue he had captured from coworkers and customers, aphorisms and observations he had made standing behind the register.

Then he line-edited the piece. He cut redundancies and tightened the prose wherever he could. Looked for any errors or sags in the narrative tension. He originally placed the bulk of the Wesley interview in the center, but after reading it through, decided Wesley's decision-making, philosophy, and strategy for the business were crucial to the story arc and needed to be introduced sooner, so he moved that section closer to the top. He made Wesley the catalyst for the piece.

Satisfied he had revised and polished the story as well as he could, he read it aloud from his desk against the back window of his room. He had managed to keep it to under 3,000 words. A little long, but he was proud of what he'd written and would fight for it if necessary.

He emailed Wesley his quotes and told him he was on a tight deadline and asked for any changes back ASAP. Wesley was up checking email that night and responded an hour later with some minor wording adjustments but nothing major.

He suggested a headline for the piece: Chain Reaction: How One Colorado Marijuana Company Broke Away From The Competition To Start A Successful Retail Empire. He crafted the email as carefully as he wrote the lede for the story, double-checked he had attached the Word document with a dozen or so photos the PR team had sent him, and sat back to consider if there was more he could do.

There wasn't. He'd done everything he could.

He hit send.

The next day Henry worked his shift in an anticipatory limbo. The day went by in a disassociated blur. At home after his shift, he bounced back and forth from checking his email on his computer to checking it on his phone for the better part of two hours. He needed to get out of the house and find a gym.

He did a trial workout in a repurposed grocery store. Artificial turf lined the floor of the front section of the gym where people flipped over tractor tires and whipped ropes up and down. The rest of the space was more traditional equipment—rows of treadmills, Stairmasters, and elliptical machines. He did light exercises, the moves the physical therapist had taught him. He tracked his progress—how many repetitions of how much weight and the number of sets per exercise—with an app on his phone.

As he reached the end of his workout, he checked an email notification from his editor who said, "This is a good start. Thank you! Will get back to you with questions and edits."

He reread the email, smiling, resisting the urge to go straight home to pour himself a celebratory drink. His anxiety shifted to whether he would be able to satisfy his editor's questions.

The following day, the edits that came in weren't overly extensive. He was asked to provide a few examples and clarify a detail or two, confirm the editor hadn't made the story factually inaccurate after rewording and condensing the language. It took him a couple of hours to go over the changes and send them back. After that the intertwined relief and fear set in. He'd done it—successfully executed a story for a national magazine. This was journalism at a high level and he had performed. This also meant the possibility for a sizable amount of attention. The potential for thousands of people to read his story in print.

Henry had the next day off, so he spent the morning trying to write a personal essay about reverse culture shock. That was coming together well—he was enjoying the freedom of not writing journalism. He worked on it deep into the afternoon until he had a 1,500-word draft he thought might be decent after a few rounds of revision. He realized if he didn't get out of the house he was going to spend his whole day off inside and it was beautiful out. Warm, the sun dazzling and familiar, the type of light he loved. He got on his bike, uncertain where he wanted to go.

People about his age sat at tables in front of a dive bar he'd heard about but hadn't visited. He went in and sat at the bar and tried to engage the old man serving drinks in conversation, but he was ignored. The jukebox played Eric Clapton low and sad and Henry worked through PBR after PBR trying his best not to be Kerouac or Cassady or some other cliché. He checked his phone—the show he wanted to see was sold out so he waited to hear whether or not Kat was busy. He wasn't sure what he would say if she texted back.

The physical therapy exercises weren't working fast enough to ease his back pain. But the painkillers and alcohol helped, and after two more beers his brain felt wrapped in gauze.

"Fuck, man," a guy in a red hooded sweatshirt two barstools down said to him, pointing at soccer on TV. "What's this fucking Spanish shit? Fucking soccer?"

Henry just said, "futbol," and shook his head. The guy asked the bartender, "Can't we put on the baseball game?"

"Don't have it," the bartender said.

"You don't have the fucking subscription service—well, suck my ass, man." He drained his beer and stood up and went over to the pool table.

Henry's back felt like the muscle was going to bow his spine backward until it snapped. He shook out a pill from a small plastic packet and chased it with his beer.

The bartender turned on a show recreating the "best" kills from the most recent war. A soldier with quarterback eye black and an M4 over his shoulder walked into a bombed-out house. "Fuck yeah get those ass suckers," the guy said.

The fake soldier on TV shot at a target from 80 yards with a bolt-action rifle and the guy said, "It's really not that impressive. Fucker had three shots to do what most people could do in one. Suck ass."

Come see me, Kat texted. *I'll meet you at the bar on the corner by my place*

Henry asked for a shot of tequila.

Then he was on a good mixture of substances, biking through the city streets, the sound of car tires on pavement, traffic flowing in streams.

When he got to her street, he fumbled with his lock until he got it figured out, then went in and sat at a corner of the bar and ordered an IPA. He had finished the first half of the beer when she came in with her hair still wet, wearing a light blue v-neck T-shirt and dark jeans.

He hugged her and said, "You smell amazing." She laughed and said, "A compliment for once?" He leaned on the bar and intently tried to get the bartender's attention, not sitting down even after she had set her purse on the bar and took a seat.

"You've been drinking," she said.

"Stopped at the bar by my house before I biked over."

"Your eyes look ... weird? Shiny."

"I found some pills I didn't know I had."

"What do you have?"

"Oxy. Want some?"

"Possibly. But let's have a drink first."

"That's what I'm trying to fucking do here. This guy." The bartender saw Henry intently staring at him and made his way over. Henry sat down next to Kat. The bartender, young, with an expertly trimmed beard and a scowl, stopped and glared at them.

"I'll have a Bulleit rye on the rocks. Double. And she'll have a ..."

"That sounds good to me."

She turned and looked at Henry. "You sure you're OK?"

"I'm celebrating. I got a story accepted."

He told her about the Sugar Magnolia piece.

"So that's why you were always taking notes. Am I in it?"

"Not this one. Maybe if I ever write a novel."

"Well, good for you. Let's celebrate." She waved the bartender back over and ordered shots. After that round, they went to another bar across the street. Coors Light beer and shots of Jameson.

"Let's go to your place," he said.

Inside her apartment, they were making out on the couch when a shock of pain went up his back and he let out a groan.

"What happened?"

"My back is still really fucked," Henry said.

They tried to make out more, but he couldn't make it work. He apologized and tried to go down on her until she told him to stop. She went to the kitchen and brought back a glass bubbler packed with marijuana. They smoked it, and Henry felt himself shrinking away from reality, his vision tunneling and his mind slowing down. He put his head back on the couch. Before he fell asleep, she said, "You should probably go."

31.

It was hot for a September night, and Taylor sat in the living room with the windows open. She was looking at her phone, relaxing after a YouTube yoga session, when she heard the marchers from a few blocks away—chanting and bullhorns and swells of cheers from the crowd. Taylor leashed Louie and went out to the sidewalk. He was sick but still wanted to walk. The first crowd that went by was mostly college-aged and not particularly organized. Police were posted at the intersection but weren't aggressively posturing as the crowd chanted, "Hands up! Don't shoot!" Taylor went to the lawn of the church and watched as more protesters passed by.

She took Louie back home and got Danielle. They went about two miles before the cops started shooting pepper balls at the crowd and they had their first taste of tear gas. They choked and sputtered until they could get home and pour milk over their eyes. The next day, a Saturday afternoon, they packed masks and ski goggles. They joined the biggest crowd yet at Civic Center Park. By the time they got there, the protesters had already coalesced on the grounds near the capitol. Another smaller crowd of counter protesters stood with signs reading BACK THE BLUE and American flags in a black and white color pattern with one blue stripe through the middle.

The march moved west past the community college campus. They chanted "Say his name!"—"Say her name!" The protesters broke into a roar as they flowed out to the westbound lane of the interstate. Taylor and Danielle were carried along and stepped onto the hot asphalt they had driven on so many times but could never imagine walking on. The march started to slow then abruptly stopped, filling in behind them like backed up traffic. Taylor could see the head of a cop on horseback pacing back and forth. The chants grew louder. "This is getting out of hand," Taylor said from under the bandanna.

"Good. These fuckers should be uncomfortable," Danielle said. She was wide-eyed, charged with energy.

A pickup with a bed full of men driving eastbound veered into the median, coming straight for the crowd. Screams of fear and people pushed to move out of the way. The police started to move to block the pickup. The truck turned alongside the marchers and the men in the box, some wearing gas masks, held weed sprayers and doused the crowd with a liquid that smelled like piss and hot sauce. The truck stopped for a few seconds until the cops on horseback approached and shouted commands with their bullhorns. As the truck drove off, Taylor recognized a couple of faces—one guy wearing a mask over his mouth with a tattoo of a cartoon frog under his eye. The protest broke up soon after. Taylor and Danielle checked their clothes and were piss-free.

The anti-police, pro-racial justice crowd was bigger the next day, and it swelled for at least a week. The marches continued and Taylor and Danielle joined when the processions came through the neighborhood. When the conflict between the protesters and the police worsened to rubber bullets and pepper spray every night, they had to close their windows or the gas would burn their eyes and make it hard to breathe from inside their apartment. It escalated to the police blinding a couple of people with pepper balls. They saw on the news that some poor guy was walking to his car, caught a stray round to the face, and lost an eye.

It came full circle for Taylor and Danielle when a security

guard protecting a TV news crew shot and killed a Proud Boy named Kevin, who they learned was the guy who used to work for them and had robbed their store. Kevin had faced off with the security guard, slapped him, and when he went to pull his canister of bear spray the guard had shot him square between the eyes. The guard would be charged with manslaughter but later let off by pleading self-defense.

32.

Henry walked down the street on a Sunday morning, birds singing in the trees. He passed the corporate pizza store where a man stood next to a shopping cart piled high with clothes, blankets, and assorted belongings. The man was eating pizzas from the dumpster and throwing the crusts on the ground. He danced to music from his phone that sounded like Van Halen, next to the crust pile he was building.

The artisanal donut shop on the corner was packed for brunch. From across the street, he thought he saw Kat standing in line with a guy in a leather jacket. A lifted pickup truck with a Punisher skull sticker on the back window revved its engine and blared its horn at a RAV-4 struggling to parallel park. When he looked again he couldn't see where Kat had gone.

Kat had quit the store to take a job running tours at a brewery in LoHi. On her last day, she had said she would text him. That was a week ago. And now he thought he was seeing her everywhere he went.

He had texted her yesterday, saying, *In your opinion, what Denver bar plays the best music?* A simple, harmless question with an obvious follow-up—do you want to go together? But she didn't respond.

His back still hadn't healed, and his Oxy prescription had

run out. He didn't have health insurance or the money to go to another doctor.

He sent a group text to Taylor and Danielle:

Hey sorry I've been MIA. Kinda got caught up with the job and seeing what this new city had to offer. We should get together soon. You two around?

Danielle texted back: *We're throwing a hotel party tonight! We didn't tell all the employees but you should definitely come! I'll send you the details.*

Henry went back to his room and took a nap then read for a while. Under the advice of his physical therapist, he did a round of planks because sit ups hurt his back. When it was time to go, he put on a faded gray denim shirt, dark gray chinos, and black desert boots. He carried his phone, vape pen, and wallet in his front pants pockets so he could ride without losing them.

It took him about 20 minutes to bike downtown. He stopped at a light and watched a hawk perched on top of a powerpole eating a snake. The bird held the snake in its talons as it stretched and tore and ripped at the reptile.

In the hotel elevator, he assessed his appearance in the silver-lit mirror. He still had most of his brown hair and the bike was keeping him in decent shape. He should probably get more sleep. He rode up to the top floor. When he stepped out, there was only one door at the end of the hallway. The thick hallway carpet muffled his footsteps. A woman in a blue dress and gold hoop earrings checked his RSVP on her phone. "Sounds lively in there," she said as she keyed in the code and opened the door.

The living room had a stocked bar manned by a bartender with bright orange spacers in his earlobes. People sat around a dining table with bowls of marijuana buds, bongs, and boxes of other cannabis products piled up on one end. A cocktail waitress in a white blouse and black skirt carried a tray with caviar on crackers. The noise from the crowd overpowered the house music.

Henry ordered a pale ale from the bartender and stepped onto the balcony. Out there, Danielle was telling the stoned, smiling group, "You really should eat before you hit concentrates. Last time I dabbed—live resin—I started dreaming I was floating in an alpine lake. I woke up on the floor with people throwing water on me. My skirt was around my chest. Not good."

Henry walked to the railing and looked out.

"There's a dab rig in the bedroom, right?" Taylor said.

"Best place for it," Danielle said. "Right next to the bed."

A guy wearing a knit hat and a T-shirt asked her, "Why Medusa?"

Danielle held her right arm out to the side and twisted it to look at the tattoo on her shoulder. "I wanted to send the clearest message possible that men should stay away from me. It never works."

Downtown, the construction cranes rose above the skyscrapers and hotels and condos. Homeless encampments spread in the city parks and on the lawns in front of government buildings. More high-rise apartments were being built all throughout the city.

Henry went back in to take a shot. At the bar, two women in tight dresses were comparing calf muscles. "This is such a leg town," the one in the sparkly gray dress said. "Everyone's hiking, biking all the time. I need to work on my arms." She flexed her bicep.

"Right," Henry said as he approached the bar. "Why wouldn't you get your leg work done outside here?" The ladies looked at him and walked away.

The bartender poured him a shot of tequila and said, "Good effort." Henry laughed. The guy said, "I picked a bad time to stop getting high. This would have been the perfect gig."

Henry took the shot over to Wesley, who was leaning backward like he was trying to escape from a bad conversation. They cheersed and Henry knocked the tequila back.

"Caviar?" Henry said. "Things must be going all right."

"Our sales strategies are paying off."

"This is the dream, right?"

"We're getting there."

Danielle came up to them, smiling, her face flushed. She said, "Are you guys fun?"

Henry looked at Wesley to see if he wanted to answer.

"No. But really. Are you?" She stuck out her tongue. A yellow square of plastic on the tip of it. She swallowed and said, "Anyone else want to microdose a little acid?"

"Not me," Wesley said. "My acid days have been over for a long time."

"I'm good," Henry said. "I need to sleep eventually tonight. I'm opening the store tomorrow."

"So the answer is no. You guys sound old. Gross."

She spun away. Henry took out his vape pen and offered it to Wesley. He shook his head.

"I used to be able to vape every day," Wesley said. "On my commute home from work. In the summer, the sun would be setting over the mountains. I'd have my music going. I'd pull out the pen. It was great. But then, one day out of nowhere, I hit my vape and seized up. Panic attack. My body twitching. Couldn't drive. Full-on freak out. Same way ever since."

"That's rough." Henry hit it and his mood changed. He thought he knew what was going to happen when he consumed THC, but it was different every time. This time it was pleasure mixed with anxiety. He hoped the latter would fade.

Taylor walked around the party with a tin of mints for the guests. "Trust me. Your breath could use some freshening up," she said to each person she approached. "Five milligrams THC and CBD."

"I had a customer ask me the other day if it was really true that weed cured cancer," Henry said to Wesley.

"Could you imagine the sales? What did you say?"

"I said 'There's not enough research at this point.'"

While Henry waited for the bathroom, a guy in a T-shirt

with a picture of Kim Jong-un, Rodrigo Duterte, and Donald Trump playing spin the bottle asked if he wanted to hit his pen.

"What's in it?"

"This one's DMT."

"Holy shit."

"It makes everything sparkle."

"Think I'll skip that for now. What do you do?"

"I'm just here for the party. Danielle hired me to show up and make sure everyone had a good time tonight. Bring my bag of tricks. My title's the Fun Manager. I'm getting business cards made."

In the bathroom, Henry sat on the toilet and made as many notes in his phone about this scene as he could. When he came out, Danielle and Taylor were standing with Wesley in the kitchen addressing the party. The music was paused and Taylor held up her glass to offer a toast to Wesley. Wesley sipped his drink and looked at the floor. Taylor glanced at Wesley and narrowed her eyes for a second, then she rushed through thanking him for his role in building the business. Henry took another shot and quietly let himself out.

Before he got on his bike he texted Kat:

Are things really better without me around?

He rode for a few blocks before his phone vibrated in his pocket. He stopped on the sidewalk and took it out.

She responded:

No. Not at all.

He sent back:

When can we get together?

He scrolled through his feeds waiting for her to reply, but she left him on Read. He biked home, the cool air stinging his eyes.

33.

___

As Henry rode to work the next morning, his phone vibrated three times in the pocket of his jeans. He locked up his bike in front of the store and checked his phone. Two push notifications from the local newspaper about the protests and one from the magazine editor. "Your article is up," it said. He clicked on the link and saw the headline: "Dispensary Dispatch: A day in the life of a marijuana retail worker." His byline in all caps and bold. Now it was out of his hands. He had walked on stage in front of a theater full of people. He'd have to wait to see how the audience responded.

Whenever he could get a break and step away from the counter he checked on the story. He went to the site's Facebook and Twitter pages to check the likes and comments it had received and he compared those to other recent features. It was performing well.

He read through the comments on social media and on the site, only feeling the negative ones. "Somebody's been reading too much Hunter Thompson," and, "Trying pretty hard to be Anthony Bourdain," and, "Not that well-written but interesting."

The article trended at the top of the most-read and most-emailed categories in the boxes on the side of the publication's home page for two days. Henry's Twitter follower count steadily rose. He had trouble focusing on work—if he had known the article would do that well, he might have taken a few days off.

At around five o'clock, he was wrapping up his shift, finishing his end-of-the-day duties, when he looked up to Taylor. She stopped in front of him and held up his article on her phone. "What the fuck is this shit?"

He finished locking the safe and turned to face her. The room had gone quiet. She was visibly trying to keep her composure, her face flickering between a fake smile and rage. "You've completely burned us. Fuck you. I thought we were friends."

"Wait, I'm sorry. Is it that bad?"

"Yes, it's that bad. Did you just take the job to spy on us?"

"Wait. Did I get anything wrong?"

"You got a lot wrong. The biggest thing was writing this in the first place. You're fired. Immediately. Jesus fucking Christ. I can't believe this."

Henry grabbed for his notebook and dropped it on the floor.

"Look, I'm sorry. I didn't mean to—"

"It was that notebook, wasn't it? What else is in there?"

"Nothing. Don't worry about it."

"Just get out of here."

He walked out to his bike and rode away. At a stoplight he checked his phone again. Several emails had come in with subject lines that were a variation of Your Story. Most were from readers, but one was from an editor at a national publication asking if he wanted to write more about the industry. What he really wanted was an agent interested in the possibility of expanding the story into a book.

Henry felt tight. Almost sick. Before the story ran, he had thought it might get him some attention. But not like this. He didn't care about the emails. He only cared about Taylor hating him now.

When he got back to his apartment he tweeted:
Well, today was my last day with Sugar Magnolia.
Any editors out there looking for freelance cannabis writing, or travel, or nature, or local climate coverage, I'm your guy.

He received one more email from a business publication that wanted him to pitch some stories for business owners, which didn't interest him much, but he needed the money and made a note to get back to her.

Earlier that afternoon, Taylor had no idea the story was out until a worker—the packaging crew manager with black hair and a tattoo of a cactus on the back of her hand—knocked on her office door and said, "You guys saw this, right?" She held up her phone with the headline of Henry's story.

Taylor glanced up and said, "Will you text that to me?" She Googled and found the piece before Steph's text came in.

She texted the link to Danielle with the message: *This is really bad.*

As soon as she finished reading it, Taylor Googled, "How to win a lawsuit against a magazine." Not so easy. She drew up a damage-control plan which included scrubbing computer hard drives and email accounts of any communication hinting at directives to promote their more-than-one-ounce-of-flower sales practices. When she went through her email she read correspondence with Danielle reminding her why they had made the decision. The subject line was Wesley's plan, and she read over it again. She had told Danielle this was going to happen. She thought up other ways to move as much flower as possible before the cops raided them—aside from trying the Nebraska market.

Taylor scanned through more email archives. She read early messages with Wesley. The tenor of the exchange from when they first started was so optimistic. They discussed the steady descent of the prices of a wholesale pound of marijuana and how to view that as an opportunity. When they first started buying off the market, a pound of decent quality flower would sell for $2,500-$3,000. But that price didn't hold. Too many growers and too many who expanded their operations efficiently meant a saturated economy. Wesley could find pounds of wholesale flower for less than two grand and even lower after the fall harvest, when the larger outdoor and greenhouse operations in the southern part of the state flooded the market.

"We can get plenty of attention by advertising the under $100 recreational ounce in Colorado," Wesley had written. "We can still keep our higher-quality bud at closer to $200, but we'll have them lined up out the door for under $100 ounces. They'll buy a few concentrates or edibles while they're here. They'll definitely buy other stuff. Lighters and pipes. The amount of attention we'll get just by putting out the less-than-$100 price alone will be worth it. It's the gas-station model. We get them to come to us for cheap gas (flower), then hope they make other purchases."

"It doesn't sound crazy," Taylor wrote back. "We all knew this was coming. I just didn't think we were already there."

"Part of our goal is to set the tone of the conversation. Not just react to it. We have to do what we can to differentiate our brand. That's how we succeed. We need to build our brand recognition. And to get people in the door."

Taylor didn't see any directly incriminating evidence, but she reflected on how easily persuaded they had been, how much they had feared the competition, and how badly they had wanted to do well. She decided not to delete the email exchange so she could prove Wesley's culpability if it ever came to that.

She called a meeting with Danielle and Wesley. Not a typical meeting, where they would ease into the business at hand with someone bringing up a funny anecdote from earlier in the day. If someone had a major life event happening—a new house, a sick family member—they might talk that over first.

No, that day, as Wesley was setting his coffee down, Danielle said, "We're fucked, aren't we?"

Taylor felt it, too, but didn't know what to say.

Wesley said, "I wouldn't quite put it that way."

"Well, how would you put it?"

"We need damage control."

"What exactly is the damage?" Taylor asked. "How would you define it?"

The room was silent.

Wesley said, "The cops or the city might raid us. If they do, we're going to lose our licenses."

"Are you fucking kidding me?" Taylor said.

"Unfortunately not."

"This was your fucking plan. Am I wrong?"

"It was not my plan to have the cops misinterpret the law. Or to hire a spy," Wesley said. "Or to lose an entire harvest in a cornfield driving a stolen van."

"What aren't you telling us?" Danielle said.

"You've been getting—I've been telling you exactly what you needed to know."

"You should've been telling us everything," Danielle said. "What else are you not saying? Did anyone ever contact you about how we were selling our flower?"

"Nothing you needed to know."

"Oh fuck that," Taylor said.

Wesley leaned back in his chair. Taylor imagined he had suspected this day was coming but not this soon.

"Give us the room, please," Taylor said.

"OK. Remember I'm going to visit my parents tomorrow."

"Oh so you're going to fuck us, then leave?" Danielle asked.

"Not how I would choose to look at it."

"I don't give a shit how you would choose to look at it," Danielle said. "Go. You're certainly doing more harm than good by staying here."

Wesley walked out with his chin up.

"Motherfucker," Taylor said.

"I should have listened to you," Danielle said.

"Are we just going to sit around and wait until we get busted?"

"What other choice do we have? We don't know what the cops are going to do. I say we try to clean up as much as we can. Stash our cash. Try to make sure we're in compliance, and just keep going." Danielle put her head on the table.

"Not much of a plan." Taylor stood up and leaned against the wall. "But I don't have a better one."

"We can make it through this," Danielle said. "Alcohol's recession-proof. Same with weed. We can make it."

"Maybe. I'm going to go talk to Henry," Taylor said. "I'll meet up with you later."

After Taylor went to the store and confronted Henry, she met Danielle at a Mexican restaurant not far from their house, where the happy hour special was a Corona and a shot of tequila for $10. The first round went down fast.

"This is so fucked up," Danielle said. She waved for the server to bring another round.

"We need to do something," Taylor said. "It's all over social media. It makes us look really bad, and the industry is going to talk. Goddammit. I'll call Haviletsky. Check on our options. But first, let's take these shots."

They got drunk on tequila and Mexican beer and picked at the chips and guacamole as they analyzed again where they had gone wrong. It came down to both of these stupid men. With Wesley they understood what he did and took some responsibility for it. They'd hired him and knew he was ambitious from the beginning. They had never really trusted him, but he'd made them a lot of money, even if they should have been suspicious of all that easy success. Henry was different, supposed to be their friend. They'd known him since they were kids. He was someone they had trusted.

34

Henry had been staring at his phone for an hour, nursing a whiskey and ginger, trying to ignore the bartender coming by to check on him. "Can I get you another drink?" and "Anything else?" He was about to send another text when Aidan finally showed up. He unshouldered a backpack a lot like Henry's and set his feet.

"Sorry, dude. Took forever to get an Uber from the airport."

"Did you shave your head?" Henry asked. The lack of hair made Aidan's dark eyes and sharp features stand out.

"In Mexico City. Too hot down there."

"Those Mexico pictures have been pretty awesome. Looks like you've been having a good run."

"It definitely looks that way. There's been some sketchy moments, too."

"You're showing up right when I'm in the middle of some shit."

"Perfect. I love doing that."

Henry told him about the job and the story. As Henry talked, Aidan sat back on his stool and waved to the bartender. He ordered a rum and coke with a lime, then Aidan turned and scanned the bar. "Now I know why they call it Menver," he said.

"If you're halfway decent and the slightest bit normal there are plenty of girls."

"Doesn't appear that way."

"Trust me."

They finished their drinks and walked over to Henry's place to drop off Aidan's bag. Henry gave him the quick tour and explained how Betty, the owner, thought of this place as her own curated salon for artists.

"Sounds like a sitcom," Aidan said. "You should write a TV show about it."

In an Uber to a neighborhood with breweries and food trucks and a lot of young people, Aidan looked out the window and asked, "You like being here?" in a way that was half-mocking, half-curious. "This enough for you? After living in Asia? You like this lifestyle?"

"So far it's been alright. But enough? Who knows?"

"How long you think you're staying?"

"Fuck, I don't know. I'd be surprised if I'm still here in six months."

"Six months is a long time. You could be anywhere."

"I'd love to stay in one place for a while."

"But where? Too many options."

"Where you going next?"

"Back to Saudi. Best money. But no girls. You should have seen the line for the 4th of July party at the U.S. Embassy. Out the door and down the block. They kept a strict 3 to 1 ratio men to women."

"Sounds like a good opportunity to get some work done."

"If I had any discipline."

"You just need to get started."

The driver pulled to the curb. They hopped out and walked up the street to a brewery with dogs on the patio and a food truck selling cubanos, muffalettas, and mac and cheese. On the other end of the beer garden, a woman in a tan dress and cowboy boots played a Tyler Childers cover on acoustic guitar.

"Let me get these beers," Aidan said as they walked up to the counter and read from the chalkboard above the bar. "I'll be making that sweet English-teaching money again soon enough."

They ordered IPAs and sat at the bar. Aidan turned in his stool and made another room scan.

"In the sandbox, the locals set up dates at the supermarket where they talk to each other on Bluetooth headsets while they fondle the produce," Aidan said. "The unmarried women can't really be seen talking to men in public. That's why I need to do some living now."

"Sounds like the absolute worst place for you."

"Could be. But dude, I'm getting tired of chasing it. That's all I've been doing since college, basically. A year of reading and playing guitar and swimming in the pool sounds fine. And when I'm done, I'll have a nice fat bank account. The plan is to start a surf school in Portugal. You should be my business partner."

"Portugal again?" Henry said, sipping on the bitter, citrus-flavored beer. "How many times have we talked about that?"

"Dude, it would be epic. Land there is still cheap. Amazing food and wine. Biggest waves in the world."

"Put together a business plan while you're in the sandbox and I'll consider it."

There wasn't enough action in the brewery and Aidan wanted to play pool, so they finished their beers and walked up the alley to a place with a fake speakeasy facade over a basement door. Inside, pool tables spread out over the floor like the rolling benches of a marijuana greenhouse. They went to the bar and put their names in for a table. While they waited for one to open up a server brought over whiskey cocktails in highball glasses.

"You mind if I text this girl I'm sort of seeing?" Henry asked.

"You do you."

When their name came up, they took a tray of balls to a red felt table and Aidan carefully racked them, pushing the pool balls forward into the triangle with his thumbs and delicately lifting it to keep the pattern tight. Henry broke, hitting the white ball with as much power as he could muster. The multicolored balls bloomed across the pale red background. Both a stripe and a solid fell. After he missed a long shot on the nine into the corner, Aidan chose solids, or spots, as he called them, and ran the table, expertly using English and cue ball placement to leave himself easy shot after easy shot.

The next game Henry fared slightly better, making about half of his balls, but Aidan made two lucky shots—a bank into the corner and a jump of some distance—and won again. Aidan took his stick with him over to a pair of women against the wall and asked if they wanted to play. He chose the prettier one for his partner—a Latina beauty with blonde hair and green eyes—Elisa. Henry's partner was pretty, too—a white girl with freckles and reddish eyebrows, hair the color of a tangerine—Courtney.

Now that he had a reason to try, Henry stepped up his game, and despite some last-minute heroics from Aidan—a three-ball combo to make the 11, another ridiculous bank shot off of two rails—Henry's team won. Aidan bought a round of tequila.

They played two more games, changing partners each time to try to figure out who was the best player. Aidan deemed Elisa the weakest, to which she laughed and leaned over the table to take another shot, saying, "When you look like this what does it matter?" When Aidan suggested they go to another bar, an izakaya-style place they had passed in the alley, the women quickly agreed.

In the dark bar with red Japanese lanterns hanging from the corners, they ate shrimp tempura and took shots of sake. Courtney and Henry were talking about music, bands they'd seen play recently, and Aidan was talking about himself, where he'd lived and traveled to, where he was going next.

Elisa laughed, making fun of him, calling him a wannabe Indiana Jones.

"I fucking love Indiana Jones," Courtney said.

"I thought you girls were too young to know who that was," Henry said.

"My older brother used to make me watch that," Elisa said. "Young Harrison Ford can get it."

With the next round of sake, Aidan and Elisa moved closer to one another. Courtney was going on at length about the medicinal benefits of ketamine. She had signed up to participate in a clinical trial and gone to two sessions so far. She said she never thought the K-hole could feel so good.

When the drinks were gone, Henry ordered an Uber XL and he got in the third row of the Chevy SUV with Courtney. Aidan and Elisa were making out before the car left the curb. Henry asked the driver to turn up the music. He and Courtney both took out their phones and rode through the city with their faces lit up by app light.

At Henry's place, they went up to the second floor. Aidan followed Elisa into the bedroom. Courtney took out a joint from her purse and asked Henry if he wanted to share. He opened his laptop and asked her what type of music she liked. "Anything," she said. "Turn it up." He hit play on a mix of his favorites.

Courtney put her hand on his leg, and Henry said, "Don't worry about it. We can just chill." She sat back, relieved, and took out her phone. Henry blew another hit toward the window.

His phone vibrated. Kat. He answered and said, "Hey! I was just thinking about you." Later he would wonder why he had answered it, why he'd said, "Sure, come by if you're in the neighborhood." For some reason, THC made it impossible for him to think about future outcomes. Until then, he had thought where he lived was too shabby and weird to have her over. But now his high brain thought it would be a good idea to invite her over when he had another girl there.

He texted his address and 20 minutes later Kat responded with: Downstairs. He went down and let her in. When they came up, Aidan and Elisa were on the couch half dressed and when Courtney saw Kat, she said, "Is this your girlfriend?" Henry laughed and relit the joint.

"Why did you tell me to come over when you had girls over?"

"I don't know. I'm high," he said. "But I did want to see you." He tried to move closer to her and give her a one-armed hug.

"You're joking," she said, sliding away.

The other two grabbed their stuff and left. Kat tapped Henry on the forehead. "Stop smoking weed." She walked out, and Henry went and sat next to Aidan on the couch.

"Was that your chick?" he asked.

"God I'm fucking stupid."

"Epic night, man. Elisa was great."

"Let's try to get some sleep."

In the morning, Aidan packed up and they walked over to a Greek diner. They sat at the counter and ate corned beef hash and drank cup after cup of coffee. Aidan used his phone to buy a flight to Las Vegas leaving later that day. He said he wanted to see if he could keep his luck going. Henry waited with him until his Uber got there, in one way jealous that he was still moving, in another, knowing the loneliness he carried.

35.

Nothing like putting a city skyline and a mountain range in the rearview mirror to gain some perspective. Wesley knew all about leaving a place to leave a feeling. He'd done it many times. But the farther he drove from Denver, the more one uneasiness was replaced with another. His parents would always appear happy to see him, even if the cannabis industry was not a business they were proud of. He was hours away from home and he could already hear his mom saying, "I'll pray for you."

The wind picked up, and gusts rocked his SUV. Not enough to push him off the road, but enough to make him hold firmly to the wheel. A piece of black weather stripping flapped up by the passenger side windshield wiper, the gusts working to peel it away from the vehicle. For a car this expensive this shouldn't be happening. He was careful not to get too close to the semis and their trailers swinging in the gusts. He looked out across the prairie and all the people this wind made crazy. The homesteaders living in holes dug out of the sides of hills, in houses made of sod, before there were any real trees here. Everything covered in dirt all the time.

At a rest stop, he held tight to the car door while he opened it. He twisted his body around as he stepped out to push it closed. He took Momo to the fenced-in dog run where the mutt sniffed and peed on the weeds until he stood at the gate, signaling he was ready to go. Wesley tied him to a sign by the brick building. A dust devil of paper scraps and plastic swirled by the entrance to the bathroom. He let it pass before going in. Inside, the smell of urinal cakes and hand sanitizer.

When he came back out, he tucked the weather stripping into the hood and used two hands to open the car door, grabbed the inside handle as soon as he opened it and pulled hard to get it shut. He drove on that straight, flat highway for two hours, listening to ambient electronic music and plotting his future, Momo sitting up in the second row looking out the window.

As he exited off the interstate, he recalled how at a party a few weeks ago a guy with his hair shaved on the sides, long on top, and a thick brown beard, had asked where he was from. Wesley told him he grew up a few hours away by car. "So, you're from the Cornlands, then," this guy said, smirking. "Right," Wesley had responded. "Something like that."

The town had prospered for decades until it began receding during the 1980s farm crisis. Wesley considered how he felt about it. He had gone through the period of post-college years where he decided this town was not the place for him and probably would not ever be. Whenever he came home, he was overcome with memories of childhood. He tried to select the best memories he could as he drove down those streets, to see in a positive way the place that made him, to be grateful to have the chance to return and process his past from a changed perspective. A chance many people his age no longer had. So many Americans move and scatter and move and scatter and have no sense of a relationship with the place where they were raised and formed. Even if Wesley never lived in this town again, it would be home for as long as his parents kept the same house he grew up in. They would be the reason he came back.

After spending years in cities, the open land had taken on a different appeal. In his Denver neighborhood, going for a walk could be stimulating—the streets buzzed with noise and life and traffic. But on the plains, the landscape expressed itself in a more understated way. For one, the sky was the real attraction here. A visitor might think this land was empty. Yet he came from this place, so he knew how to identify the subtle variations and patterns. He could put words to what he saw. There, a red-tailed hawk perched atop a power pole scanned for voles. There, two dozen round bales cast slanting shadows on a field of cut alfalfa. There, a full-grown, white and gray Charolais bull grazed on short pasture grass, his muscles defined around his hump. He knew the names for all of it.

It was about five o'clock when he drove up his parents' street. The houses in the neighborhood were spaced out with cottonwoods and honey locust trees and well-maintained front yards. When he parked and stepped out, the familiar, sweetly rotten smell of the sugar factory conjured up a flood of memories, so many and all at once. He let them pass. He turned off the car and sat in silence. He prepared himself for his parents' questions and gentle, nudging advice, especially from his mother. He resolved to be as patient and positive as he could. He let Momo into the backyard and watched him trot down the fenceline.

The front door was familiar and comforting. Its handle and weight. The way the spring squeaked as it closed behind him. He stepped in and set his suitcase inside the door. "Hi, Mom," he said. She was sitting at the kitchen table reading what he guessed was historical fiction. Her hair was the same tawny brown as Wesley's, straight and medium-length. She wore reading glasses, a loose pink blouse, and dark gray stretch pants. She hugged him, smelling of rosewater, and asked about the drive. "Windy," was all Wesley said.

He went to see his dad. He was in the living room watching a nature documentary in the same blue recliner he had sat in for years, his plaid shirt and jeans pressed and clean. Older each time Wesley came home, his hair white, reminding Wesley if he could settle down and start a family, his father could be a grandpa.

"Did you finally come home?" his dad asked. "I thought you forgot where we lived."

"Just for a few days."

"Well, that's not very long." Wesley shook his hand and smelled his spiced aftershave. He sat on the couch and turned toward the TV. His mom took the chair next to his dad.

"So are you tired of the city yet?" his dad asked.

"Not quite."

"And just what are you doing now?" his mom asked. "I know you're working."

"I told you guys—I've been helping run a business. A legal cannabis company."

"Oh," his mom said. "I thought you said you were starting a 'candle' company. That's what I told everyone you were doing. Making candles."

"Nope. Cannabis. We're selling marijuana. You know it's legal there now. A lot of people buying it."

"Well, I hope you're at least making some money," his dad said.

"The company I'm working for is actually doing really well. I'm just not really seeing eye-to-eye with the owners."

"Your dad knows about that industry. He goes online a lot more than I do. I check Facebook. But he's better at the computer than I am. Speaking of that, can you look at this? It keeps popping up."

Wesley helped her fix a problem with the anti-virus software on her laptop. The conversation slowed down until they were all sitting there watching snow leopards chase goats down cliffs somewhere in Asia. He texted Holly.

Hey! I'm in town. Are you busy? Want to meet at Mary's?

Yes! Can we go now? (three beer mug emojis) John can take the kids for a little bit.

20 minutes

"I'm going to meet up with Holly. I'll be back later."

"Now?" his dad said. "You just got here."

"I haven't seen her in forever. We're just going down to Mary's. We can all do something tomorrow."

"Bright and early," his dad said. "I need you to help me with some tree branches."

When he walked into Mary's, Holly was at the bar with half of a red beer—Bud Light and tomato juice—sitting in front of her. Wesley didn't recognize anyone immediately, which came as a relief. He hugged Holly and they told each other they looked good. Wesley genuinely meant it. Holly had three kids but appeared basically the same as she did in college. Tall and strong. Longish, curly hair with blonde highlights. Clear skin. Gray-green eyes. She was wearing a fashionable black top with jeans and new Adidas sneakers. She liked to dress up but couldn't overdo it. He appreciated that she didn't ask the questions, "What's life like in the big city?" or "How can you stand all those people and all that traffic?" Those were questions people their parents' age asked. And Holly knew the answers. She had lived in Los Angeles after college, working in fashion, before she came home to take over her mom's bridal shop and clothing boutique. Wesley didn't have to ask if Holly missed the city or if she enjoyed being a mom—the answer was yes to both. Best friends since they were 14, they had stayed close through the separation adulthood demanded, commenting on each others' social media posts, sending private messages and texts, keeping their friendship going as best they could. Throughout his 20s, Wesley hadn't found a better, more loyal or trustworthy friend. And even if Holly's life was prosaic now, calm and routine, Wesley recognized how much strength the stability gave her. He ordered a whiskey and ginger and another red beer for Holly.

"How's the pot—I mean *cannabis* company?"

"Honestly it's kind of a shit show."

"Really. It sounds so interesting. Denver seems to suit you."

"Does it? Half the time I want to pack everything up and go live out in the country."

"Overrated. You'd get bored pretty quick."

The bar was filling up with a mix of older regulars and a few younger farmers and ranchers and people who worked in town. Wesley tried not to look around too much, though he was curious who he knew. It started to get loud. The jukebox played modern country. They tried to update each other on the gossip they had—people they'd seen around lately, if anyone had gotten married or divorced, sick with cancer or died. None of it was said in a judgmental way, merely passing information. Wesley was genuinely curious how his old hometown friends were doing. For the most part, it sounded like everyone was doing fine. Holly finished her beer and shouldered her bag.

"I have to get home. Bedtime for the kiddos."

"Already?"

A hand on his shoulder and a "Hey, man. Didn't know you were back." Carrick Williams was there in a camouflage Pioneer cap and a tan hooded Carhartt coat, jeans and boots. Wesley stood and gave him a hug. A faint odor of engine oil.

"Hey, Holly," Carrick said with a nod.

"Hey! I was just leaving. You can have this spot." She hugged Wesley around the shoulders and said, "Good to see you. You two have fun."

Carrick leaned on the bar and looked over the booze. "You don't want a shot, do you?"

"I shouldn't. Cops are probably out."

"The cops are always out. It's early. You'll be fine."

"You want to go somewhere else? I've been here a while."

"All right. But first." Carrick ordered two shots of tequila.

Carrick's truck was surprisingly clean. Wesley expected Mountain Dew bottles half filled with chew spit and a dusty dashboard—fast food sacks on the floor. But it was tidy. Three Black Ice tree air fresheners swung from the rearview mirror.

Carrick played the local country music station on the radio as they drove west out of town.

Wesley had once known Carrick like a brother. In high school, they were so well-suited for friendship that when they were learning how to drive they would go out around town and cruise, not saying a word to each other for hours, listening to music and watching the town go by. Learning from what they saw of the world. Then Carrick had his trouble after high school and Wesley was in college, and they didn't each see each other for years. But none of that changed the bond they had.

"So how's Denver?" Carrick asked.

"Pretty fun."

"Better you than me. I was over there a couple of weeks ago. Downtown seemed bad. What are they calling it, urban camping?"

"Oh yeah, that's getting worse."

Carrick drove them up to the canal road and they parked where they could look out over the town.

"Sometimes I'm jealous of you guys," Wesley said. "This seems good. Easier."

Carrick glanced at him and took a drink of his beer. "It's not simple, I'll tell you that. We were wrong when we thought we knew what it was like for our parents."

Wesley searched for any landmarks he could recognize. Tried to find his parents' street among the flickering lights.

"I'm thinking about starting my own business," Wesley said.

"Also better you than me. I tried that once. About destroyed my life."

Carrick put in a dip of chew and offered Wesley the can. The lights on the airport tower blinked red.

"Remember when we climbed on top of that?" Wesley said.

"And Molly got scared? Just froze up there, wouldn't go up or down?"

"Thought we were going to have to call for help."

Wesley asked how Ethan Thomas was doing. Carrick said he was still in town, somehow. "He seems to like it," Carrick said. "He's good at the newspaper job."

"I don't know how he does it. Writing every day in a community where everyone knows you. Seems horrific. But good for him."

"So you're good?"

"Yeah."

"Happy?"

"I don't know. I'm fine."

"You should come back. It's not so bad."

When they'd gone through the updates it got quiet. They didn't like talking about themselves that much.

When Wesley got back to his parents' house, the whole place was dark, but he could find his room blindfolded. He stepped around the spots in the floor that creaked so he wouldn't wake his parents. In his childhood bed, he thought about what he was doing with his life, and whether or not he could come back here to live. The past isn't a foreign country, it's your hometown, he thought, and it's always there waiting to remind you of who you were, asking what you've made of yourself in spite of what it made of you. The people he cared about were more important to him than anything, and that meant Holly, and Carrick, but it also meant his parents. They didn't have much to talk about today. They would if he came home to live, to get married and start a family. He may not have career options here, but he could start his own thing. There were enough people in town to make a business work. The thoughts came as a surprise. He hadn't confronted those ideas before. He thought maybe it was time to make an exit from Sugar Magnolia.

In the morning, he pulled onto Main Street driving south. As he passed the Starting Line diner in the fake old train car, a sheriff's patrol cruiser turned in behind him. He watched in the mirror as the cop drove up closer to get a read on his out-of-state plates. The cop followed him all the way to the edge of town then turned around. Wesley decided to sell the SUV. He'd need the money.

Back in his Denver apartment, he sat with his laptop and composed an email to Danielle and Taylor. He considered writing a formal resignation letter, but this wasn't that kind of job, so he simply wrote:

Hey Danielle and Taylor,

I've given this a lot of thought, and I'm officially resigning from Sugar Magnolia. This has been an interesting experience, and I've learned a lot. Thank you for the opportunity. I wish you all the best.

Sincerely,

Wesley

He took Momo out for a walk, thinking about what moving back home might feel like.

36.

Henry woke up hungover and hungry. He biked to the corner deli that sold fancy meats and cheeses to grab a sandwich and a coffee. The sun was warm and the air mild. He went in and there Kat stood in the back room, chatting with a guy who appeared to be running the wine shop, the same guy Henry might've seen her having brunch with. There weren't any customers back there and she was speaking quietly to him, smiling, her hand on his arm. She wore a black leather jacket with silver zippers that opened to a white T-shirt. She looked well; she was laughing at his jokes.

Henry considered turning around and walking out, saving himself any potential awkwardness. He was still feeling raw and stupid about what happened with her at his place when Aidan visited, but he told himself not to be a coward, that if he started running away now where would he stop? Kat didn't have any more right to this place, or any other place, than he did. Maybe she'd come over and they'd have a chance to talk. He ordered a toasted turkey and avocado sandwich from the counter. By the time he was done paying, he turned to look and she was gone.

That afternoon, he was at a coffee shop on the corner, drinking tea and reading *Under the Volcano*, when he got an email notification on his phone:

BACK TO THE FUTURE SPACE JAM @ EXTRACT-ED REACTION

The Green Dahlias welcome you to the most bitchin', the most totally tubular, the raddest of the rad '80s-themed space cannabis dance party. We're going to party like it's 1989...on the moon!!!! Tonight. 7 p.m.

He went home, got cleaned up, and rode his bike down to what the hipsters called RiNo, with its factories and garages and machine shops converted into breweries and art galleries and ramen joints.

He locked the bike to a rack in front of a warehouse decorated with a string of light bulbs draped over the front patio. An armed security guard checked his ID, and a skinny, stoned guy wearing amber sunglasses and a shiny red leisure suit pulled up his invite on an iPad and gave him a handmade program. "Some sick vendors in there, bro," he told Henry. "Tons of dope swag."

Inside, people in costumes milled around in a fog of cannabis smoke. A handful of booths ringed the space, and the map on the program showed an empty box next to each business. The instructions said attendees were to take a picture or video of each booth, tag the event and the company on a social media post, show the booth worker the post and have them stamp the program. Filled with stamps, the map could be turned in for a goodie bag full of marijuana products.

Not seeing anyone he knew at the party, Henry participated in the activity, picking up a free joint here, an infused chocolate-covered-coffee-bean there. He took a shot of CBD grapefruit juice. A woman in a full-body, acid-washed denim suit and a mirror-ball helmet put a drop of THC honey on his tongue. He asked each vendor for their Instagram handle, shot a short IG story video, had his booklet stamped, then moved on.

A few of his posts received emoji reactions—flames or raised hands or party hats with confetti. When he collected all the stamps, he turned in his card for the swag bag and stood at a high-top table next to a counter filled with snacks—Cheetos, Doritos, fruits and vegetables, cookies and pastries. The bag contained a box of marijuana chocolates, a pack of rolling papers, a vape pen, a T-shirt and socks, and a mini dab rig.

In one corner of the warehouse space, a pair of DJs played electronic dance music from computers on a banquet table. A few women in shiny silver cosmonaut suits and purple wigs danced with muscular, athletic movements, all these beautiful young women into the weed and the music, dancing and smiling and happy. He tried the vape pen—tasted like fake mango and petroleum. He took pictures and a couple of videos to help with details if he decided to write about it later. If he needed more inspiration or imagery he only had to search for the relevant hashtags on Instagram. #spacecannabisdanceparty #greendahliasdodenver #marijuanaonthemoon

Smoking potent pot made him feel like he needed to piss. When he went looking for the bathroom, Henry opened a door to a low-lit den with slow, ambient music and purple light, five people sitting on a couch with a pile of white and gray mushrooms on the table. Four of the five people talking at the same time. The one not speaking was Wesley, who watched him. Henry apologized and backed away.

"No, no, no," the group said as one. "Come in. Come in. Come in."

He went in and sat in a short chair at the end of the table. Wesley handed him a mushroom with a blue stem and white cap and said, "Here. I'm abstaining, but you go ahead."

"I can't. I have a sinus infection," Henry said. He hit a joint and tried to interject himself into the conversation, but the excited voices were an impenetrable wall. Each simultaneously talking about themselves, rapidly firing off anecdotes and analysis, laughing before the punchlines, the subject of the conversation changing so quickly there was no point in attempting to contribute.

Wesley leaned over and said, "I'm leaving Sugar Magnolia. But you should know the owners hate your ass now."

"Where are you going?"

"Was it worth it? That article paid you what? Five hundred bucks?"

"I was trying to tell the truth."

"Get the fuck out of here. You think what you wrote was the truth? You didn't understand what you were writing about."

Henry stood and they all turned their attention to him, a four-headed chattering couch making comments about his clothes and shoes and teasing him for leaving. He rode through a beautiful, cool, fall night in a city with life and sound and possibilities, but he couldn't enjoy it. He was thinking about Taylor and Danielle, about how it all had gone bad, and how much of it was his fault.

When he got back to the house, Chuck D was sitting cross-legged in a chair in the living room listening to Lou Reed, wearing a pink thrift store dress, bright blue eye make-up, and holding a goblet of red wine.

"Well well well it's the writer," he said, smiling. He sat up. "How's your night going?"

"Fuck," Henry said and fell onto the couch. He noticed how dirty it was—crumbs and dog hair. Crusty stains. He took a gold-plated CBD vape pen from the goodie bag and hit it, the tip turning a bright pink.

"Writing the Great American Novel, I see," Chuck said.

"Not now, dude."

"Jesus Christ, I wonder how much art has been lost in this city to a cloud of vape smoke, of legal fucking weed?" Chuck sat up.

"C'mon. At least I'm not bored."

"But pot is soooo boring. It makes people really boring. So nice and calm and locked inside themselves. Way more the 'opiate of the masses' than religion. When weed is completely legal just watch how much dumber we become. Peace and love and a populace with stupid grins on its face getting preyed upon by the sober predators." He held up his wine. "I prefer chaos, if I'm honest. Every time I get high I just wanna be alone with food and music. All my problems come to the surface. I end up remembering some high school trauma I hadn't thought about in years."

"Yep. That's exactly what's happening up here right now." Henry tapped his temple.

"That shit's buried, and I don't want to dig it up. I want to build a fucking building on top of it. But hey, if this conversations is boring to you, don't mind me."

"Got a lot on my mind. Sorry."

"Go to bed. G'luck with your 'novel.'"

Henry went to his room and wrote a bad, undercooked poem about Kat then fell asleep and dreamed of being trapped inside a hotel where all the balconies were missing their floors.

37.

Wesley packed his apartment into a U-Haul storage pod and left it on the curb for the company to ship out later that day. It was September 11th, and when he got on the interstate the giant American flag in the mousetrap interchange was flying at half mast, the wind stiff enough to blow it crisp and straight. He took I-76 headed northeast, his city life fading away as the miles accumulated. Momo sat on the front seat next to him.

He had a lot to think about and plenty of time to do it. He was determined he wasn't finished with the cannabis industry. The U.S. marijuana market was projected to be worth billions, and if he could work his contacts in the more established companies that were interested in multi-state expansion he might earn a good living. He could write applications for business licensees, consult on grow operations, and become an executive in another company as he had with Sugar Magnolia. That's how he'd sell his story to prospective employers—he'd learned what he needed to in Colorado and now he was bringing that knowledge to help build the markets in other states.

He pulled off the interstate for gas. He let Momo out to pee in a sugar beet field next to the parking lot, then he went to the truck stop diner and sat at the counter for a cup of coffee. A hulking man with a tattered blue T-shirt and red suspenders two stools down read a newspaper and forked up a piece of lemon meringue pie. Wesley scrolled through his phone, checking feeds and emails. The man put down his fork and set the paper on the counter, tilted back his foam and mesh hat.

"I'll tell you," he said, in Wesley's general direction. "This used to be a helluva country. Now it's just shit."

Wesley thumbed his phone and looked up to see if the server was bringing his coffee.

"I remember when we talked to each other. Now we just have our little dumb phones and live in our own little worlds. Christ."

Wesley went back to his phone.

"Just exactly what I mean. We all forgot how to talk to each other."

"Except for you, Slim," the woman with the apron said. "You haven't lost the gift of gab."

The waitress set a white cup in front of Wesley and filled it with coffee. The Key Lime pie in the case looked good so he ordered a piece. When Slim saw him put down his phone to eat they had a friendly conversation about climate change— "a hoax," according to Slim, gun reform—"another form of government control," abortion—"here's what it says in the Bible about when life starts," marijuana legalization—"are you shitting me?" and liberal cities—"should all be burned to the ground. Start over." He said, "This whole thing went to shit when those damn Arabs supposebly flew those planes into those buildings. If you believe that really happened. Been gone to shit ever since." Wesley listened politely until he was done with his pie. He asked for a to-go cup and took his coffee and got back on the road.

The horizon served as a comforting fixed-point to stare at, and while the scenery seemed tranquil and static at first glance, the longer he watched it the more he saw. A herd of antelope grazed in a wheat field on the horizon. In the middle distance, a red tractor and baler slowly rolled over alfalfa. The hatch opened and a green round bale fell softly onto the cut field. Above, a flock of unidentifiable birds flapped their wings westward. Might've been Sandhills cranes.

The drive was uneventful, familiar, flat, the road straight and clear. At his parents' house he ate dinner with his mom and dad and when they retired to the family room to watch TV, he brought his bags up to his old room and sat at his school desk. He thought about calling Holly and Carrick but he could do that later. On his laptop, he searched for "fake news image" and saved to his desktop a picture of a pile of newspapers with EXTRA! EXTRA! VERY FAKE NEWS! as the only headline. He posted it to Facebook with the caption: Never believe everything you read. There's always more to the story. Ignore the haters and the judgers and the people who think they know the whole situation. They don't. Do you. Let them talk.

The post picked up 112 likes and hearts, with the comments #beabadass and, "Fuck what other people think," and, "I tell my kids all the time 'who do you need to worry about?' I think it's the best advice I can give them." A person he hadn't spoken with in years asked, "I agree, but what's this about?" Wesley declined to answer.

He checked his phone: Seven missed calls and voicemails from numbers with Colorado area codes. He would listen to the messages in the morning. When his parents were asleep, he went out to the yard and lit a blunt and puffed it until the cherry burned red. His phone vibrated in his pocket. Haviletsky. Time to discuss his options, he figured. Wesley saw this saga ending with him ordered to turn in to a Colorado jail for at least a couple of weeks. Probably probation. That didn't bother him much. He'd expected to do a little time. The street cred might help his reputation. But for now, he was content to be home again. The stars and the way it all smelled felt right. He'd call the lawyer tomorrow.

38.

Henry was reading about the new coronavirus when his phone buzzed. A text from Kat:

Hey how's life? :)

Before he responded, he finished reading the guidance from the World Health Organization. It sounded bad, but he had no idea.

Hey, it's been a while! he wrote back.

He watched the three dots in the speech balloon as she crafted her response.

It has! I was wondering if you wanted to meet up for a drink? If we can still do that?

Sure. We can find a patio somewhere. When's good?

Tonight?

They sat at a sidewalk table of a cocktail bar on Tennyson.

"What happened to you?" Henry asked. "You disappeared."

Kat paused. "I knew you were going to ask that. I needed to figure something out."

"Did I see you at the butcher shop in our neighborhood? Do you have a boyfriend?"

"That's what I was figuring out," she looked over his shoulder then back at him. "Figured out that guy was an asshole."

From the open garage door windows they could see inside. The bartenders wore blue and white Hawaiian shirts. One danced as he rattled his silver metal shaker over his shoulder. A couple sat down at the table diagonal from them in a muffled exhalation of energy. Henry recognized the early excitement of two young people who genuinely liked each other. They appeared to be on a date, but it wasn't the awkward lack of chemistry of an online stranger meet-up. They knew each other. Grinning and laughing as the other spoke. When there was a break in the conversation, Henry heard them talking about their traveling plans getting canceled. The guy said, "I had plane tickets to go to Japan." Kat glanced at Henry and sipped her drink. The girl said, "I was going to Thailand!"

Henry laughed and said, "And here I thought traveling in Asia made me special. If I decide to move back, do you want to meet me over there?"

"Maybe. I do want to stay here. I'm actually having fun. I like America. I think I'm a masochist."

The couple stopped talking, intensely staring at each other, before getting up to leave. The bartender came by holding two tall pink drinks with watermelon rinds for garnishes.

"You two want these daiquiris? That couple ordered them but apparently had to leave. Plague-free, guaranteed. On the house." He set them down and patted the table.

"You look better," Kat said, sipping the drink. "Are you still taking oxy?"

"Nah. Prescription ran out. Thankfully. That shit's bad." Henry tried the cocktail. Shook his head. "Too sweet for me."

"Let's not drink these," she said. "Let's go back to my place." She stood up and put some cash on the bar and he followed her out.

It began as soon as they got in the door. Kat pressed him against the wall. "What's wrong with this belt," she said. She undid his fly and he did the same to her.

"I've been thinking about this," he said. He knelt. Kat took her foot out of her pants and placed her heel on his shoulder. Henry counted as she held his hair. When he got to a hundred he stood.

Kat pulled the elastic of his boxers out far enough to take them down. She paid back the favor. Henry put a hand on the wall to steady himself.

They went to the floor. "Did you stop running?" she asked. "You seem a little loose." The wood floor hurt his knees, so he lifted himself onto his toes and elbows, going as fast as he could until he almost lost it. Her hair smelled like beer. He slowed way down, counting to ten as he went in, a move he had learned with someone else. He did that for a moment then rolled over. Kat got on top and put her feet flat on the floor as she moved up and down. He tried not to make eye contact. They weren't there yet, it was just fun—love could come later. They were just two people who liked each other. Kat put her hand on herself and arched her back until her eyes closed and her breath caught and her face flushed. Henry put his hands under her thighs and lifted her off, shuddering, turning his head, embarrassed. She rolled over next to him. He stared at the ceiling, wanting to get up to turn off the overhead light, but he also didn't want to move. She went in the bathroom and wet a washcloth and gave it to him, then she shuffled over to the speaker on the nightstand and turned on some music.

He spent the night, and, in the morning, Kat told him she wanted him to go camping with her.

"I'll drive," she said. "The car's already packed."

The interstate curved through the Rocky Mountains west of Denver, with mountain peaks layered like purple construction paper. Most of America's major freeways avoided the beautiful places—not the case here. Henry felt pretty damn certain he'd never be able to buy one of the log cabin-style mansions on top of a mountain. Even if he had the money, why would he buy a house in the woods when the forests were always on fire now? He should just enjoy the view, but it all made him sad. He turned his focus to the driver.

She was cute, wearing a headband and light makeup and sunglasses, the stop-and-go traffic stressing her out. He tried the radio, but the signal would cut out when they dropped down the other side of a mountain, so he connected his phone to Bluetooth and played a Nathaniel Rateliff album.

She had made a camping reservation months ago, probably to go with the other guy he'd seen her with, but what could Henry say about that. He could never plan far enough ahead to make camping reservations, so he'd take what he could get. He thought of himself as outdoorsy, even if he owned no real gear to do any outdoorsy activities. He had owned a tent and a sleeping bag but gave them away with the rest of his belongings when he left the country the last time.

Their reserved spot was at the back of the campground loop. People were out next to their tents and campers grilling hot dogs and burgers on charcoal grills. Kids rode bikes through the grounds. Henry and Kat spread out the tent on the designated pad tucked away back from the picnic table and fire pit. Their campsite smelled of sagebrush, smoke, and the nearby vault toilet when the door to the bathroom opened. Henry laid out the canvas footprint, connected it to the tent, snapped together the two sets of aluminum poles, and hooked the tent to the poles. He hammered the stakes through gravel and dry dirt with the flat end of a hatchet. He hit one of the stakes crooked and it bent.

"You're like lightning," Kat said, poking him in the ribs as she passed by with their bedding. "Never strike the same place twice."

He draped the rain fly over the tent and staked it down. Kat crawled inside and blew up their sleeping mats. When the tent, mats, and sleeping bags were all arranged they gathered dry twigs and needles from the forest around them. After a few trips into the forest, he had a pile to last them through the night. Despite the restrictions, they were still allowed to build a fire in the designated pit. Henry stacked the pieces of firewood in a cone shape over the wadded up paper and kindling. He grabbed at the lighter. "Let me do that."

"What are you, the Keeper of the Fire?" She held it away from him.

"No. I just had it arranged so I could hit it with the lighter right where I wanted and it should go."

"Okay, Boy Scout." She handed him the lighter.

The fire started the way he planned it. He opened the cooler and fished out two icy, sour beers from a brewery in Longmont. They cracked the beers, tapped them together, then went to work making their lunch. Henry set up a two-burner Coleman gas stove on the picnic table. Kat wiped out the cast-iron skillet with a paper towel. She had packed a chicken curry and a can of beef, carrot, and potato soup. They heated up the curry first and settled by the food, drinking their beer and waiting on the stove.

"So what's next?" Kat asked.

"I have this joint if you want. But I was thinking that would be good around the fire after dinner."

"No, I mean what's next for your life?"

"Good question. I think I want to try freelancing for a while. I mean, I think I have to."

"Oh god. Full-time freelancing sucks. I tried that for a year. I almost went crazy. Pitching indifferent editors. Filing quarterly taxes. Taking shitty assignments. Eating ramen noodles for every meal. It's really hard."

"I've wanted to try it for a long time. See if it works for me."

"I'll take an assignment here and there when they're offered, but I'd rather have a steady paycheck and do freelance projects on the side. Video editing. Some producing. It works better for me to have a job and freelance on the side."

Before they had left Kat's apartment, she had talked about the camping trip as an escape from technology and told him to grab a book from her shelf. She strung a canvas and nylon hammock between two aspens and lay in it to read from Celeste Ng's latest, and Henry sat at the picnic table with *A Pilgrim at Tinker Creek*. They made it through one beer and a few pages before they decided to set the books aside, connect the speaker to a phone, and play music while they drank. "This is the Colorado life you'd see on a TV commercial," Henry said. "I'm alright with it.

As dusk settled in the temperature dropped. They peered west from the picnic table while the shadows grew, the white sky turning dark. The moon rose pink, nearly full. They put on lightweight layers and located their headlamps before it got dark. Kat heated up the stew and they ate it with plastic spoons. Dessert was graham crackers and chocolate with marshmallows roasted over the flames. The sweets didn't go well with the sour beer. They switched to a boxed pinot noir. Henry pulled out a narrow plastic tube, popped the cap, and shook out a joint.

"One of my last remaining Sugar Magnolia pre-rolls. A sativa. Super Silver Haze. Says twenty-two percent."

"I'm going to take one or two hits. Any more and I have an out-of-body experience."

Henry lit it and took the first three drags. Kat coughed when she hit it. Then they quieted down and breathed in the forest air. From the speaker, the lyrics came out clear, the meaning easy to grasp. The wind shifted and the campfire smoke swirled around them. The fire cast shadows up into the trees. When they stared at the flames too long, it took a minute before they could really see the stars. If they were patient, they had a clearing above them with a view of a streak of the Milky Way and partial constellations.

"I need to get my own place," Henry said. "This time hopefully without bed bugs."

"Good luck. Housing is ridiculously expensive now."

Henry leaned back in his camp chair. As his eyes adjusted, a satellite tracked across the sky.

"Colorado really isn't a bad place to live," he said.

"Agree. It's not Thailand, but it's pretty good. Plus you can't leave me. I need my new camping/reading/wine buddy."

When the firewood was gone, they picked up around the campsite and brushed their teeth with water from Kat's water bottle. The tent sex was slightly challenging until they moved the inflatable mats to the side and just used the blankets. Hard on the knees but more stable. After, Henry lay there listening to the forest insects, Kat rustling on her mat as she got settled. A feeling of calm. He fell asleep to the sounds of the woods creaking and Kat's gentle snuffling.

A group of drunks arrived at the campsite next to theirs after midnight. Henry could hear every shuffle of feet, every door slam, every dropped cooler, every inane comment. For what seemed like hours, they dragged gear out of their cars laughing, telling bad jokes, one guy giggling at every dumb utterance. Henry got up and asked them to keep it down.

"I don't care about you," one guy said. "I don't know you." But the group eventually passed out and quieted down.

When his alarm went off at 5 a.m., Henry was groggy, but waking up in the forest among the birds and insects and trees gave him energy. He and Kat quietly moved around the campsite, putting on hiking boots and eating granola bars and brushing their teeth, the mood peaceful, expectant.

"I would stretch," Kat said, screwing the lid on her Nalgene. "And drink as much water as you can."

"Should I be nervous?" Henry asked. He stuffed a waterproof jacket into an orange backpack Kat had lent him.

"Nah. Nothing to worry about," Kat said. "Just a long walk."

Shadows retreated across the highway as they drove toward the trailhead. The sun rose somewhere beyond the mountains to the east, giving off a pale light, rays curving over the edge of the earth. They drove parallel to a meadow, the radio off, wind against the windows and the tires on the road. A herd of elk grazed in the distance. The turn to the trailhead led them back into the forest, with cars parked in camping spots dispersed along a creek, tents and hammocks under the trees. About two dozen cars filled the parking area.

People adjusted gear sitting in their SUV hatches, leashed their dogs, stretched for the hike, and slammed their car doors. Henry zipped up his fleece and switched on his headlamp. He put on his backpack with water bottles, energy bars, and his phone, and they started up the trail.

Before he got injured, Henry had been in the phase some men go through when they spend a lot of time in the gym lifting weights, trying to transcend the narrow frame his genetics had provided, willing his way into a different physique. It had sort of worked. He had put on about 20 pounds of muscle, much of it in his back and shoulders. But his lungs weren't in great shape for the altitude and thin air.

Kat was a naturally gifted athlete, a high school track star, nimble and quick. She set the pace. Henry pushed himself to stay with her.

As they hiked up the gradual slope toward the tree line, the easiest part of the day, Henry could already tell he would struggle to keep up. He'd be watching her summit the mountain well ahead of him, and in another 20 minutes, Kat indeed pulled away, Henry jealous of her light-footed pace. He had wanted a girl he could do these types of activities with. He had found someone much better at them.

The sun cleared the treetops and cast the trail in shadowy light. The first hours through the forest were gradual and pleasant. Cool. Easy going. That changed as they reached the rocks, moving into thinner air and a steeper grade, the trees behind them, nothing to block the sun overhead. Kat wasn't bothered by the change in terrain and atmosphere. She shrank as she put more distance between them, both of them finding their own pace. Henry struggled with the lack of oxygen at this altitude, his lungs heaving, burning. Mouth open, legs heavy.

After an hour above treeline, he sat on a rock and dug out a bar of chocolate and peanuts. His stomach both cramped and unstable, in the early stages of a growing nausea he would carry with him up the mountain. It would only get harder until they summited and started back down. In a way, he enjoyed the fight. It made him only focus on a single purpose, to simply put one foot in front of the other, to will his way up the mountain—forced meditation, all he could think about.

In another way, he was straight up suffering. He now also wanted to vomit. Each step on the trail made the feeling worse. Altitude sickness felt like being out on a rough sea for hours. His head was telling him he had fallen ill and should stop and turn around.

He paused to drink water. He could barely see Kat up there, a dot on the trail. He wanted to speed up, but he couldn't will himself to do it. He sat on a rock to gather himself. A gray-bearded old man wearing a hat with ear flaps came up slowly and stopped next to him.

"You look like I feel," the old wizard said, leaning on his hiking poles. He had an amused gleam in his eye and red cheeks. "A little green in the gills."

"I'm going to puke," Henry said. "I feel like I'm seasick."

"That might mean you're overdoing it."

"Probably, but I want to get this over with."

"It's beautiful up here. Look at the views," the old man said and hobbled away.

Henry looked at the rough-hewn mountain tops around them, the two alpine lakes on the peak adjacent, the way the trees changed to a lighter color as the elevation increased until they gave way to stone. The mountain peaks were partially covered in snow as though a painter had brushed white paint on the rocks then left to paint somewhere else, leaving swaths of violet stone uncovered. Lower down the mountains the white streaks ended, and the peaks were chopped down, lower and lower, the sides deep green and pale purple. The sky over the landscape glowed neon blue, flickering in Henry's vision.

Henry thought he could make out some elk down in the

valley, but nothing moved. His back felt like it was trying to push his ribs up through his chest. He regretted having quit the painkillers, but if he could finish the hike without them he could do anything. He wanted to go back down—he also didn't want to lose his chance with Kat. He wanted to impress her, or at least show her he had the resolve to finish.

He stood and willed himself forward using two methods. The first: He settled on a point farther up the trail and fixated on it, plodding toward it one step at a time. Eventually this method was too easily cheated and stopped working. So he began to count his steps. He would push to 100 then pause, out of breath, dizzy, his stomach in his throat. Once he recovered he began again.

In this way, he overtook the first false summit, then the second. On the last stretch, in the thinnest air, he could only go 50 steps at a time before pausing.

At treeline, the sun had been shining and it was relatively warm. Now, snow fell in soft pellets. Other hikers gained on him, others were on their descent, and a few in worse condition. One step at a time, Henry summited the mountain.

He stumbled over to Kat who was sitting huddled in a half circle of boulders sheltering her against the wind. It was below freezing and the frozen rain pellets stung his face. "You made it." She was hugging herself and rubbing her arms.

"Barely. Thanks for waiting. That was the hardest thing I've ever done."

"You're really pale. Are you OK?"

"I'll be fine."

They picked up a piece of cardboard with 14,439' written on it. They asked another hiker to take their picture with Kat's phone, drank some water, ate a Clif Bar, and began their descent.

Once he started descending, Henry felt immediately better. With each step down the mountain the pressure in his stomach lessened. His brain stopped trying to signal to his body he was sick and he should stop. He no longer felt like puking, could walk quickly now, no counting, a quick pace to the treeline, which promised cover and a break from the wind.

What a privilege to spend a day walking up and down a mountain for entertainment. Yet, Henry also liked the accomplishment that came with this outing, the challenge. He wanted conquests, no matter how incremental or trivial. He was pleased he didn't fail, and he'd get a nice dopamine hit when he posted this to social media as soon as he was in an area with a cell phone signal.

"Do you ever think going overseas was a mistake?" Kat asked. He could keep pace with her now that they were headed down.

"I mean, when we were over there, it wasn't very good here. So our timing was fine. But yeah, I don't know. Some of my friends here bought houses after the market tanked, when the government was giving out loans, and now their property is worth way more. They started families. They have a lot more stuff than I do. If that's what you want, I guess." His legs were heavy, and the downhill hike strained his knees, but his head was clearer. "Some of my friends got upside down on their houses, too. A lot got chewed up by America."

Kat was wincing as she walked. "I think I'm going to lose a toenail. I hear you though. I hate this status pressure. What kind of car you drive. How big your house is. It's all money. That's not how I define myself."

He passed Kat the vape pen, and took a hit after her. They were traveling down the mountain on sore feet and knees, worn out from the trail and relaxed.

39.

Taylor sat on the bumper of her SUV and tied her boot-laces. Her gray socks were pulled halfway up her shins. It was a weekday, so the trailhead parking lot was only partially full. Half the spots were taken up by Toyota pickups and Subaru SUVs and some smaller cars. The air was clean, the sky bright blue.

"Jesus, how many samples did we bring?" She held up Danielle's full backpack.

"Enough to get us up and down the mountain. We'll be fine." Danielle grabbed the pack from Taylor and took out a bar of dark chocolate, wrapped like a convenience store candy bar. She broke off two pieces. "This is actually really good chocolate," she said. She started a note file in her phone. "Let's see how we feel in 45 minutes."

The trail began gradually in short grass, and soon they were among fir and spruce trees on a steep incline. Danielle was more fit—she liked to take a 10-milligram THC edible and go on ten-mile runs. It helped her with focus and the pain. Taylor biked infrequently, but she was naturally strong despite her thin frame and could be athletic when she wanted ed.

The point of all of this, why Danielle had suggested they

do it, was to bring back some sense of normal, fun activity to their lives. They had been obsessing over Henry's story and Wesley's departure to the point that was all they were doing. Danielle had said, "Let's go do something. Get outside." Before Danielle had moved to Colorado she had envisioned doing a lot of this, along with camping and skiing and generally spending her free time up here. That largely hadn't happened. They had spent most of their time building the business. But by combining work—testing samples from growers and extractors who wanted Sugar Magnolia to sell their products—with this hiking excursion, they were taking advantage of the place they paid a premium to live in, and they could write off any costs as work-related expenses.

"Do we really want to wait until the edibles kick in?" Taylor asked. "Let's see one of those vape pens."

A black-capped chickadee sang its lilting, three-note song. Danielle produced a narrow box with a black vaporizer pen inside. She made a note: "Elegant, discreet packaging. Classy." She puffed and passed it on.

Taylor drew on the pen and the tip lit up a bluish purple. "Tastes like fake pineapple terpenes." She passed it back to Danielle, who was stretching out a calf muscle on a fallen log. She took another hit and nodded in agreement. "Not great."

Danielle put it back in her pack and added to the note—Blue Dot Vapes: Packaging - A, Taste - C.

"Do you feel anything?" Taylor asked.

"Standard head high," Danielle said, stretching out her other leg. "Pretty nice, really."

"Agree," Taylor said.

"Effect - A."

Danielle walked on quietly, listening to the trees creak overhead and her boots crunch on the path. It was cool in the forest shade. As the edible started to work, a warm sensation spread through her body. Her scalp tightened and the edges of her eyes itched. "My chocolate is kicking in," she said.

"Hard to tell since we hit the pen," Taylor said. "But I'm feeling pretty stoned."

"Look at the way the light comes through the trees," Danielle said, pointing up the trail. "The forest is alive. The trees are talking to each other. Everything is interconnected."

"You're definitely high."

Danielle shook out a joint from a plastic tube. "Let's keep going. Sativa hybrid, it says. Strain: Ghost Train Haze. THC: 23.2 percent. From a co-op of craft growers up by Nederland." She lit the cannabis cigarette and took two puffs. She made a new note. "Tastes like limes and flowers. Decent quality for a pre-roll. Must be flower, not trim." At this point, the forest felt comforting, as though it was protecting her.

Taylor hit it and coughed. "Oh, now I'm officially stoned. That's good. Seems fresh? Doesn't taste like pesticides."

Danielle took another hit. "I'm getting a lot of citrus. Definitely has a shit ton of flavor." She noted their comments then put the joint back in the tube. She passed Taylor a bottle of water. A blue jay flitted into a nearby bush. Pine squirrels scurried in the underbrush. Danielle became aware of the air she breathed, its temperature and humidity, how it traveled from the path and the trees and the sky into her lungs and out again.

"Do you feel that?" Taylor asked.

"I'm really fucking high, if that's what you mean."

"Not just that. It feels like—like something's watching us."

"That's the weed."

"Did you read about the mountain lions in Boulder?"

"Are you trying to freak us the fuck out?"

"They say for every time you've seen a mountain lion they've seen you a hundred—."

"Stop."

"Can we turn around?"

"We're not even halfway."

"I don't want to die in the forest."

"Fine."

They descended quickly, punishing their knees, skipping down the trail until it flattened out.

"Give all these products an F," Taylor said. "Got too high."

They sat in the car and turned on the radio. Neither wanted to drive. Danielle scanned through the stations and stopped when they heard the voice they had listened to in the van when they almost got arrested. He was still talking about mental health and guns. Another mass shooting and an ammo shortage.

"Oh shit," Taylor said. She was looking at the transcription of a voice mail on her phone. "We just got a message from a detective with the Denver police department."

"Oh fuck."

"Should I call him back?"

"Probably not. Let's check with Haviletsky."

"Good idea."

They sat there for a minute trying to process what they should do.

"Fuck this, let's go," Danielle said.

She drove them down slowly, the radio off, the scenery beautiful. A bull moose silently trudged through a meadow, the sun lighting up the fuzz on his antlers. The leaves on the trees of an aspen forest shimmered in the breeze—bright green coins jangling in the sunlight.

They drove into a town that was once another mining camp. Now, it was all hotels and restaurants and gift shops—quintessential modern tourist mountain town. They parked in front of a brewery where the label mascot was a cartoon gold miner with a long white beard and a pickaxe.

"I stopped shaking," Taylor said. "Finally."

"Some food and a beer should help."

The bar was lively and dark. They took a booth against the wall. The server was cute and friendly and quickly brought them waters. They ordered nachos and wheat beers. They were waiting for their food when Danielle said, "No fucking way."

She slammed her hand on the table and got up before Taylor—who was slouched on the bench against the wall—could say, "What?"

Danielle went over to Henry Kaufman just as he finished cheersing the girl he was with.

"What the fuck are you doing here?" Danielle said.

"Hey, Danielle," Henry said, exhausted and scared. "You know Kat. We just got done hiking Mount Elbert. Stopped to celebrate."

"Oh, I thought maybe you were celebrating how you fucked us over?" she said. She turned to Kat. "Or did he not mention that?"

"I thought it was a good read," Kat said, leaning back.

"Yeah, well, this guy's a fucking asshole. Be careful. That's how he treats his friends. I can only imagine the shit he'll pull with you."

"Hey, I told Taylor I was sorry. I didn't realize that story was going to go—"

Taylor came up and tried to throw her water in Henry's face, but it went everywhere, a lot of it on the floor. "We gave you a fucking job, dude." Henry wiped at his face and neck with his napkin.

"All right," he said. "Fine. You guys hate me. I get it." He stood and laid some cash on the table. Kat looked annoyed, if not entertained.

"This is hilarious," Kat said. "You two are so dramatic."

"Fuck both of you," Taylor said.

"Sounds like you're the one that got fucked," Kat said. "Did it hurt? Or did you like it?"

"Hey," Henry said. "Be nice. It was my fault."

Danielle lunged at Henry and Taylor grabbed her to hold her back.

"We're leaving," Henry said.

Taylor and Danielle watched them go. When they got

back to their table their hefeweizens were sitting next to a mound of green chile and chicken nachos.

40.

Danielle turned down Jason Street with its brick industrial buildings and semi-trucks in the parking lots. She braked for a forklift loading a stack of metal tubing onto a flatbed trailer. With her window down, traffic from the freeway gave off a low hum, the air fragrant with oil and marijuana plants. A veil of haze clung to the white and gray mountain tops on the horizon. She parked in her reserved spot and walked up to Nick guarding the front door.

"Good morning," he said. "Scootch in through the front." He seemed to be on edge, even more than normal.

Taylor was in her office with the door closed. In the past few days, she had only come out for major crises that needed her attention, and when she did, she quickly lost her patience for the small problems the trimmers and growers failed to solve on their own.

The a.m. shift workers shuffled in from the backdoor as usual—a few early, a few on time, dressed for working in the warehouse in street clothes—jeans and sneakers and hooded sweatshirts, wearing the white N95 masks the company provided. Danielle left her office door open. She checked her email as the noise and energy built up out in the reception area. Deliveries came in from the loading dock, with drivers ringing the doorbell to be checked in then signing off on the clipboard. Their manifests were brought to Danielle for price checks and signatures on infused products and whole-sale flower shipments.

Midway through the morning, the front doorbell rang in an obnoxious staccato burst followed by a loud, sustained knocking. On her monitor, Danielle watched two Denver police officers at the front door. That wasn't altogether unusu-al—they popped by occasionally for what they called compli-ance checks—but she saw they had Nick sat on the curb in the street, his hands zip-tied. Her phone lit up from the store in RiNo, then the store in the Highlands, then the ones on Santa Fe and Evans. Danielle could see Taylor standing in her office, also looking at her phone. A stream of at least a half dozen policemen filed in and spread out, announcing, "Den-ver police, don't move. Everyone stay right where you are."

She went out and stood next to Taylor. "Is this really hap-pening right now?" she said.

An officer approached them. Danielle had the feeling of watching the scene from out of her body, no sound, only the police officer holding up a piece of paper she thought might read "warrant," his mouth moving, but she couldn't hear him. Then another cop was there with metal handcuffs standing behind her, and if she indeed wasn't processing the sound, the sharp steel on her wrists cut through to her separated self and brought her back into her body. She had just been handcuffed, and therefore arrested, for the first time. What an odd feeling. Scared and helpless and alive all at the same time. And now what would happen? She had lost control, re-strained by this man, by the law, and by the city and state. And how strange to see it happening to Taylor next to her, and the other employees as well, lined up in the lobby. This machine of work and industry and business they had built all brought to an immediate stop.

An officer interviewed the workers, asked for IDs, wrote down their information. The employees stared at her and

Taylor from across the warehouse. A few cried. A policeman read her Miranda rights and she wanted to say, "What a cliché. We all know this. What is this television? Nice *Law & Order* voice," but she was stunned into silence.

She heard "Let's go" and felt a push. Then she was outside in the bright Colorado sun. In that moment she could only think of how garish, how unbearably intense the light shone on the other buildings. She squinted at the men from the warehouse across the street, the siding company guys, standing there smoking, watching, cracking jokes. She counted five police cars and a military-style tactical vehicle with big wheels and either a water cannon or a gun on the top. A hand pushed her head down, and she was in the back of the still, silent cop car.

As she sat in the cruiser—presumably waiting for the police to finish rounding everyone else up—she thought of her father. The man she barely knew, who caused her mother so much trouble, who had sat in the back of many cop cars like this in his life. She had been taught to condemn him for never being around, but she felt his presence there next to her. As a kid, this city took up plenty of space in her imagination. Mostly because her dad lived in it, and at least once, though her mother thought Danielle too young to remember, they drove through the streets of this city searching for him. Danielle remembered it as around the same time her grandmother died, and, in her imprecise memory, her mother had used that as a reason to try to find him. She couldn't ask her mom about it, forbidden to speak of him, so she seized on that memory, trying to understand why she held onto it with everything she could have remembered, until it grew and grew in her mind. Although her father died when she was in high school, she still thought of him when she passed a group of day laborers in a department store parking lot or homeless men hanging out in a city park. She now knew the powerlessness he and every other person like him had felt—the same steel on their wrists, the same scratched plexiglass, the same squawking police radio. Her father sat next to her with his glasses and mustache and bright purple satin jacket, his hands also cuffed behind his back.

"My baby girl," he said. He leaned back into the seat. "Now you're in the life. Now you're getting to know your father. Now you're really my daughter. Ah, ah ah."

He was comfortable in his handcuffs. She could smell his aftershave and it made her nauseous. "Hey! Hey!" she yelled, but the cops standing outside by another car only watched her through their sunglasses and wouldn't move. "Hey, I'm going to be sick!" One sauntered over. "Let me out," she said. The officer strolled around to her door and her dad said, "Mwah, love you, baby," and when the door opened the sun burst in and he disappeared.

"Don't get it on the car," the cop said.

"Kiss my ass," she said, spitting but holding the puke in. "Let us go."

The cop walked away, and she was left there alone. Above her, the sound of buzzing, and she leaned out to see a drone hovering overhead. The camera lens in the center of the whirring machine reflected light back at her. Then she was in it, seeing what it saw, and from four hundred feet in the sky, the police cars and the tactical vehicle were strewn in a haphazard array, and the trucks in the docks of the neighboring warehouses, the trains in the yard. She thought of a boy playing with his toys on the carpet in a house, and how he might arrange them like this if he wanted to play police. Pick me up and get me out of here. Put me back in my hometown, in a different time, before this one, and we can play family, or student, or anything at all. Just save me from this. The boy went into the other room, looking to do something else, someone else to play with.

41.

—————————————

When Kat arrived at the scene, the cops had a few dozen employees lined up on the sidewalk. A pair of officers worked the line, one from each end, writing down names. From a distance, she saw the two owners led out of the warehouse in handcuffs and stuffed into separate police cruisers.

Kat's assignment was to capture drone footage of the raid and get B reel of Sugar Magnolia's marijuana grow facility. The news station wanted fresh images for weeks of future coverage as the case played out, and its helicopter crew was busy covering wildfires and protests at the capitol. Kat's freelance assignment was to provide. She was on a text thread with the station's producers and reporters that buzzed as the police simultaneously raided the dozen or so Sugar Magnolia stores across Denver. Budtenders were arrested. Signs on the doors notifying the public the shops were shuttered. Police strung caution tape around the buildings.

She controlled the drone from the street. The machine flew over the police cruiser with one of the owners in it. It looked to her like Danielle Garcia. What was she feeling, Kat wondered. To have built a business so successful, to employ hundreds of people, to be making good money, to be realizing a dream, only to have it torn away from you? And in such a spectacular, public way.

Kat tilted the camera away from the warehouses toward the mountains. She'd edit the footage later, but she liked the way the light spread over the Rockies. The right combination of weather to create a pattern where the clouds look iridescent in the sunset, the closest the landlocked place ever got to any semblance of the sea. She let the drone hover and whir far up into the sky.

When the video feed started to flicker, she had flown it almost out of range. She brought it back and pivoted the camera down toward the raid scene. Officers hauled out computer hard drives and laptops and file cabinets and boxes full of papers. This was it for Sugar Magnolia. The owners had flown their own machine too high, lost the signal and crashed.

She called the drone in, then rushed to a coworking space next to the sporting goods store by the river. She drank nitro coffee and edited the video as quickly as she could. She emailed the footage and waited to hear back.

42.

There it was, right there on the TV. From his barstool, Henry couldn't hear the broadcast, but the chyron on the bottom of the screen read, "12 budtenders arrested after year-long sting." The anchor, with her pointed, librarian-style glasses and styled dark brown hair was trapped in the glass box talking without sound, her face moving under the static and sour faces suspended above her. The arrested budtenders appeared to be in their 20s, about half women and half men, and they hadn't gotten particularly done up for work. The men unshaven, the women without much makeup compared to the woman reading the news. All of it glowing out from above the bar. Henry recognized a few faces.

His pint glass of session IPA was half gone. The couple six feet away from him was making out. The guy somehow simultaneously slid his hand up the girl's shirt while ordering an Uber on his phone with his other hand up behind her head.

Henry turned back to the TV. He felt bad for Taylor and Danielle. There was no way to really know if the article he had written had caused any of this, but it certainly hadn't helped. And now their business, and possibly their lives, had been destroyed. He assumed they would probably get light, white-collar-crime sentences and be back in the weed business soon enough, with tons of street cred to bank on. Still, they had to be freaking out.

He sent them a group text:

Hey Taylor and Dani

I know you both hate me

I get that

But I just wanted you to know that I'm sorry if my story contributed to any of this at all. I never wanted that to happen

He could see the three dots, the ... of someone typing a reply and he wanted to get out what he had to say.

You both are amazing, and I still consider you some of my best friends. I truly didn't know the impact that story would have. I didn't think that many people would read it

The bubble with the three dots disappeared, and instead Taylor just used the Thumbs Down reaction on each of Henry's texts.

Danielle responded with:

That's weak as fuck. I don't accept it.

I mean it. I never meant to cause you any harm

Henry was setting his phone back down when Kat texted him a link to the *Denver Daily News* story with an emoji of a face with two surprised eyes.

12 budtenders busted in citywide pot shop raid

Denver police today arrested a dozen budtenders who work for cannabis retailer Sugar Magnolia and suspended 30 of the company's business licenses.

Sugar Magnolia owns 15 retail stores in the city as well as cultivation and processing licenses for selling and producing medical and recreational cannabis. All stores are closed indefinitely, according to a release from the Marijuana Enforcement Division.

This is the largest profile bust since legal recreational cannabis sales began in Colorado in 2014.

The employees have been charged with selling more than the legal limit of marijuana to one person in one day. Colorado recreational marijuana regulations set a purchasing limit of one ounce per person per transaction, but the law doesn't set a limit for an amount per day.

According to court documents obtained by the Denver Daily News, several budtenders have been charged with felonies for allegedly selling more than four ounces to one customer in the same day. Others have been charged with misdemeanors for allegedly selling more than one ounce but less than four.

Multiple calls and emails to Sugar Magnolia representatives were not returned as of press time.

The arrests are the result of a year-long investigation into a practice dubbed "looping," where a customer visits a dispensary, buys an ounce, takes it off the property, typically to a nearby parked car, then returns to the store to make another purchase, amassing a substantial quantity of cannabis flower to be resold.

"Licensed marijuana rules and regulations are meant to be followed," said Shelly Guilfoyle, MED director, in a release. "For public safety reasons, compliance will be strictly enforced."

As part of the investigation, Denver police detectives both videoed several instances of people allegedly engaged in looping as well as made multiple purchases of one ounce in one day themselves. The court documents state detectives observed one person make up to 16 one-ounce purchases in one day from the same Sugar Magnolia store. The police then made contact with the buyers and in some cases allegedly found up to a pound of legal Colorado marijuana in their cars.

Many buyers were from out of state, including from Texas, Kansas and Florida, states without legal adult-use marijuana programs.

So far, neither of the owners of Sugar Magnolia — Taylor Hobson or Danielle Garcia — have been charged with any crimes.

The story also included a slide show of mugshots of each budtender, captioned with their charges and what store they worked for. An aerial video, shot by drone, was also credited to Kat.

Henry sent her a text:

Great job with that Sugar Magnolia video.

She responded with: *Should we celebrate?*

I could be up for that. I feel bad for Taylor and Danielle though.

Let's have a drink anyway.

As he biked over, Henry wondered why the cops never came after him. As a budtender, he'd sold as much flower as those other employees. He must've gotten lucky to get out when he did.

He clicked his screen to locked, put the phone in his pocket, and left the bar. He thought about what Taylor and Danielle were going through. He imagined they felt themselves victims of a society that wanted to say it was progressive, but they'd learned it was only willing to take half measures. It had sort of legalized marijuana, yet wanted to control who sold it and how. He could rent a car and drive over to a liquor store right now and fill it completely full of the strongest booze they had and no one would stop him. He could rent a U-Haul and do that. Stay drunk for months. But not marijuana. Selling too much too fast was not allowed. And now the livelihoods of dozens, if not more, were ruined. The government liked keeping poor people and people of color in jail. He figured he should probably write that story next.

Henry passed a pair of men standing in front of an apartment building quickly sharing a joint back and forth. The cloud Henry stepped through carried the aroma of black pepper and a runover skunk. The chaos of it all, the story, the jobs, the back with the misplaced ribs and the painkillers, a bank account constantly at zero. Why did he feel the need to stay in America? Any other time he would have probably decided to move on. Try another place. But then there was Kat, who had just texted: *I'm at the bar. You know which one. Come find me.* 🤍

43.

____

Taylor tilted forward on the couch, her face drawn, frowning. Danielle sat cross-legged on the living room rug turned toward the TV with the news anchors talking about the bust. It was the night after the raid. They'd called Haviletsky and he got them out of jail hours after they'd been brought in.

Danielle held a glass dab rig like a piece of scientific lab equipment, a twisted beaker. She fired up the torch, heated the nail, held her hand over it until it cooled to the right temperature, dropped a gold spot of live resin on the nail, capped it and drew up the smoke, straightening her posture as she inhaled. Her green eyes fixated on a spot across the room and her mouth open, the face of someone experiencing release. She exhaled a cloud of white fumes.

"Shit. I keep asking this, but what do we do now?" she said into the haze. Taylor didn't have any answers, but Danielle asked anyway. Her eyes were clear with a rim of red around the edges. She arched her back and supported herself with her hands. "Just how screwed are we?"

Haviletsky had said the cops were trying to build a conspiracy against them by interrogating the budtenders first—trying to get them to turn on the owners and say it was their idea to sell the multiple, cheap ounces. They both knew these minimum-wage employees had no reason to be loyal to them. Their only real hope was a few might hate the cops enough to keep their mouths shut. But the police had brought in so many on serious charges that likely wouldn't matter. And they still hadn't connected the dots on the stolen van.

"Give me that," Taylor said. Danielle handed the rig to her. Taylor took the torch from the table and went through the same ritual. She coughed. "I would say we're only as fucked as the state chooses to fuck us. Which could be pretty fucked."

"Wesley's plan."

"Henry screwed us, too."

Danielle stretched her arms across the rug in child's pose. "You know what's happening right now, right? The cops have the budtenders in some little room with a naked lightbulb hanging over a table trying to get them to snitch on us."

Taylor took another hit from the rig. "We still have plenty of business to take care of."

"But not tonight." Taylor handed the glass to Danielle.

"No, tonight we get really stoned."

Danielle exhaled and the smoke went up through the ceiling, above their house, and floated into the night, over their street and their neighborhood and the city downtown with its glass buildings and above the mountains and over the plains and the rivers and the farms and the country, this America, where despite everything the people dream of making one big score, one smart play and everything will be better and they'll have money and be happy and free and loved by everyone and they dream and dream and dream.

Acknowledgments

All the thanks to Adam Gnade, a true friend who has been there from the start, always up for a first read and to give honest feedback. Without him I wouldn't have met Nate Perkins, and without Nate I wouldn't have my publisher and my books in one of the finest bookstores and coffee shops in the American West, Trident Booksellers and Cafe in Boulder, Colorado. You two are always at the top of the list. Big thank yous for reading early manuscripts of this also go out to Wendy Fox, Neko Catanzaro, Sam Segrist, Kate Lavin, and Bram Riddlebarger — all great writers in their own right, and you should read them. And my love and sincerest appreciation always to Nammin Kim for all she does for our family, the most important project that we started together more than a decade ago. I wouldn't want to do any of it without you.

Bart Schaneman lives in Seoul, where he works as a breaking news editor for *The Washington Post*. Prior to that, he spent seven years working from Colorado as a reporter and editor on the cannabis beat.